Cricket, Fiction and Nation

Rod Edmond

ANTHEM PRESS

Anthem Press
An imprint of Wimbledon Publishing Company
www.anthempress.com

This edition first published in UK and USA 2026
by ANTHEM PRESS
75–76 Blackfriars Road, London SE1 8HA, UK
or PO Box 9779, London SW19 7ZG, UK
and
244 Madison Ave #116, New York, NY 10016, USA

British Library Cataloguing-in-Publication Data
A catalogue record for this book is available from the British Library.

Library of Congress Cataloging-in-Publication Data: 2025908641
A catalog record for this book has been requested.

ISBN-13: 978-1-83999-645-0 (Hbk)/ 978-1-83999-646-7 (Pbk)
ISBN-10: 1-83999-645-5 (Hbk)/ 1-83999-646-3 (Pbk)

Cover Credit: Military Convalescence, Hurlingham July 1917.
Hutton Archive. Getty Images.

This title is also available as an eBook.

The English are not a very spiritual people, so they invented cricket to give them some idea of eternity.

– George Bernard Shaw

Cricket is an Indian game accidentally discovered by the English.

– Ashis Nandy

In memory of my father, Donald McLeod Edmond (1916–2009), who nurtured my love of cricket, and to my son, Jo Edmond Harman-McGowan, who replenished that love.

CONTENTS

INTRODUCTION

My father had a small shelf of cricket books. Most of them were 'books of the tour', a common form of cricket writing in the days of sea voyages and long tours when teams visiting England would play every single county, the MCC, Oxford and Cambridge, an invitation team such as H. D. G. Leveson-Gower's XI and even sometimes Minor Counties or Combined Services. My favourite among his books was Alan W. Mitchell's *Cricket Companions: The Story of the 1949 New Zealand Tour*, with a foreword by HRH the Duke of Edinburgh. Walter Hadlee's team of 15 amateur cricketers arrived in April and sailed home in September, having played 33 first-class matches and a couple more of the Leveson-Gower sort. I also read and re-read the tour books of the Australian cricket writer and broadcaster Johnny Moyes, which were grouped together on my father's bookshelf and appeared with the regularity of a chiming clock. I loved the uniform pattern of these books: match-by-match accounts, scorecards of each game, summaries of how each player had performed on the tour and the camaraderie I could imagine developing over these prolonged tours.

The really odd one in my father's collection was E. W. Swanton's *Best Cricket Stories* (1953), an anthology of cricket fiction. Why make up a cricket story, I wondered, when there were so many real-life matches to be described? The stories were strange, the characters odd and the settings quaint to a lad growing up on the outskirts of a New Zealand dairy town in the 1950s. Mike Brearley describes coming across Hugh De Sélincourt's classic *The Cricket Match* (1924) at the age of 10 or 11 as a 'revelation'. Before this, he had no idea there could actually be a **story** about the game he was already obsessed with. My response to cricket fiction was grumpier. But I was a dogged reader and slowly came to enjoy Swanton's collection, to appreciate the comedy and vivid characterisation of its stories even though some of their features remained a bit obscure. And as books read in childhood do, it lingered with me.

When I began to plan this book, the stories in Swanton's collection flooded back and helped shape my project. I found it was only one of several such collections and probably not the best of them. John Bright-Holmes' *Lord and Commons: Cricket in Novels and Stories* (1988), for example, is more comprehensive. But it was Swanton's I kept turning back to, not solely for its contents but because of the look and feel of the book, its cover and its typeface, the memories it revived.

As I read more widely in the classic cricket fiction of the years either side of the First World War – the great period of this genre – I realised that the assumed cosiness of the English cricket story has been exaggerated. An archetypal village cricket story like De Sélincourt's *The Cricket Match* goes beyond the merely bucolic and picturesque to consider the consequences of the First World War, offering a picture not only of time standing still but also the effects of time passing, its erosions as well as those things it preserves. Even its contemporary, the public school story, though confined to an enclosed and entitled world, was aware of disturbances in the world beyond its ivy-clad walls and even had a few of its own. In the best of these stories, the apparent permanence of the world of the village and the public school, with cricket as its emblem and guarantor, is also picking up unsettling noises from off-stage. The invocation of any ideal tends to summon its shadow. Most of the cricket fiction discussed in this book is about so much more than cricket.

Cricket, Fiction and Nation traces the historic arc of cricket and fiction from its beginnings in the early nineteenth century, through its emergence in the early twentieth century as a form that produced some great writing, even winning prestigious literary prizes, to its decline into standardised genre fiction in the later years of the twentieth century, and its striking rejuvenation in the post-colonial and global world of the twenty-first as a revived form of serious literature. From Mr Pickwick at Dingley Dell, E. M. Forster's Maurice at Penge and the conclusion of a cricket match marking the end of Western civilisation in R. C. Sherrif's *The Hopkins Manuscript*, to the dazzling brilliance of Shehan Karunatilaka's post-colonial novel *Chinaman*, I explore the historical, cultural and psychological range of cricket fiction across its several centuries.

Cricket, more than any other sport I think, has always been a realm of stories, its fiction extending to almost any subject imaginable: from war, death, nation, class and empire to race, post-colonialism, migration and globalisation; from fathers and sons, love, sexuality and gender to comedy, tragedy, suicide, obsession, absurdity and the end-times. These themes, as well as several lesser ones – curious bowling actions, for example – provide the through-lines that give this book its shape, its argument and illustrate the multifaceted history of cricket and fiction.

A major reason why cricket and fiction have proved so readily amenable is their similarities in shape and form: the extended but time-bound nature of both; the divisions into which they seem naturally to fall – chapters or parts in fiction, separate innings in cricket; the similarities of pacing and rhythm as their narratives build towards a conclusion. The form of the murder story, as we see in Chapter 3, is for these reasons particularly well suited to cricket narratives. Karunatilaka's *Chinaman* uses a five-part structure taken directly from a game of cricket to give form and shape to the inventive exuberance of his novel. Short story form and the one-day game, as demonstrated by fiction of the village green, public school and the ODI are similarly compatible. T20 cricket, however, seems too abbreviated and single-paced to offer much to the writer.

For over a century, the dominant theme of cricket fiction was with England as a nation and the part the game has played in defining, expressing and defending national identity and imperial culture. In recent decades, however, cricket fiction has spread far beyond the country that created and for so long defined the genre. The emergence of the postcolonial cricket novel discussed in the later chapters of this book speaks of and from a cosmopolitan global world that is currently redefining many aspects of both the game and its fiction.

As I write, the 2024 T20 World Cup is underway. India and Pakistan are about to face each other at a 34,000-seater drop-in stadium in New York watched by countless millions of TV viewers around the world. Who, even at the beginning of the twenty-first century, would have imagined such a scene to be possible? Well, a novelist did, Joseph O'Neill in *Netherland* (2008). Cricket and fiction have had a long, complex and ever-changing relationship with each other, which this book sets out to explore.

Chapter 1

THE RISE AND FALL OF THE VILLAGE CRICKET STORY

The test of a true cricketer is that he shall prefer village cricket to 'good' cricket [...] the informal village game where everyone plays in braces, where the blacksmith is liable to be called away in mid-innings on an urgent job, and sometimes, about the time when the light begins to fail, a ball driven for four kills a rabbit on the boundary.

–George Orwell

Having, the other day, once again spent an afternoon in watching a village cricket match, I am again perplexed by the passion for that game which is displayed by those who cannot shine at it. They cannot bat, they cannot bowl, they leave their place in the field, they miss catches, they fumble returns; and yet, every Saturday, there they are, often in perfect flannels, ready to fail once more.

–E. V. Lucas

My favourite opening and closing scenes in cricket fiction both come from A. G. Macdonell's *England, Their England* (1933). A motley team of metro-politan writers, publishers and ring-ins, based on an actual team of the period, 'The Invalids', are playing away in the fictional Kent village of Fordenden. Macdonell sets the scene with affectionately satiric exaggeration. It is a perfect summer's afternoon.

Blue and green dragonflies played at hide-and-seek among the this-tledown, and a pair of swans flew overhead. An ancient man leaned on a scythe [...] a magpie flapped lazily across the meadows. The parson shook hands with the squire. Doves cooed. The haze flickered. The world stood still.

Fordenden lose the toss and range themselves across a field picturesquely scattered with daisies and buttercups, thistledown and clumps of dark-red sorrel. Their opening bowler, the village blacksmith of course, tightens his belt, flexes his 'terrific bowling arm', and walks back to his mark. The end from which he's to bowl slopes away so abruptly that it's only in the final yards of his approach that he becomes visible to the batsman. The opener takes his guard and looks around, surprised that no bowler is in sight. Suddenly the blacksmith comes thundering over the crest 'like a mettlesome combination of Vulcan and Venus Anadyomene', which roughly parses as a blacksmith arising from the sea. The delivery is a high-velocity wide full toss to leg, which rockets first bounce into the hedge behind the keeper. The home umpire reluctantly signals four byes, and the row of watching gaffers sitting on a bench outside the Three Horseshoes shake their heads and call for more pints of old-and-mild.

The final over of the match combines the two scenes of potential misunderstanding in cricket most likely to end in farce: when running between the wickets, especially if there's a third runner involved, and when several fielders converge on a high catch. The scores are level, and the ninth wicket has just fallen. The last man in is the blacksmith, limping heavily from a fall while bowling and leaning on the shoulder of the village baker who is to run for him. He lashes his first ball straight up into the air to an enormous height where it 'seemed to hang motionless, poised like a hawk'. Down on the pitch, confusion reigns. The blacksmith forgets his sprained ankle and sets out for the other end. So too does the baker, both men shouting at the non-striker to come on, which he does, and all three, their eyes turned upwards, meet mid-pitch with a 'magnificent clang'. Meanwhile, the fielding captain calls to one of his men to take the catch, remembers this man has dropped a sitter earlier in the innings and shouts to another of his fielders to take it instead. Both men converge obediently on the spot in the middle of the pitch where the ball seems likely to land. Other fielders become involved in the confusion, and a tangle of bodies ensues. Finally, the ball descends, cannons off someone's head and bounces on to the massive hind-quarters of the wicketkeeper, from where it is grabbed by one of the ring-ins, Mr Shakespeare Pollock, a visiting American journalist, who has been hovering around shouting baseball cries and has no idea what is happening. The batters and the runner, shaking off the effects of their fall, pick themselves up and run madly for the same end. But it's too late anyway. The catch has been taken, and the match is a tie.

Pelham Warner, writing in 1922, described village cricket as representing the essence of the game; 'for a village match is the truest democracy [...] [encouraging] [...] feelings of freemasonry, camaraderie and *esprit de corps*. I cannot imagine a man who has been bowled out by the village blacksmith not having a fellow feeling towards him afterwards. Can you imagine a cricketer becoming a Lenin?'

Another powerful figure in cricket administration of this time, Lord Harris, writing in *The Cricketer Annual 1924–25*, declared that cricketers were 'something more than participants in a game, we are the ministers of a high moral and educational medium'.

The First World War had reinforced the association of cricket with England's green and pleasant land, a setting in which the stable time-honoured social order of the nation was best celebrated. Village cricket fiction of the period between the wars is commonly seen as endorsing this understanding of the game, complacently nostalgic at a time of revolutions in Europe and labour unrest at home. But the relation between this genre and the period in which it flourished is more complicated. Macdonell's village cricket match is a riot of comic disorder ending in chaos and, as the exuberant tone of the narrative suggests, none the worse for this. It's the film the Marx Brothers never made, *A Day at the Cricket* with Harpo playing Shakespeare Pollock. And elsewhere in the novel, the Great War and its aftermath cast a shadow over the countryside.

England, Their England is a genial satire of English society in the years following the First World War, as seen through the eyes of a young Scotsman, Donald Cameron, recently recovered from the effects of shell shock, who is researching a book about the character of the English. He knows nothing of cricket. Turning out for the Invalids is part of his fieldwork, a search for that 'Team Spirit' which is said to characterise the national game. The experience leaves him none the wiser.

Macdonell was at pains to distinguish his novel from the spate of writing about the First World War that was appearing in the late 1920s and early 1930s. On the opening page, he reassures us that 'no one need be afraid that this is a war book', but in fact *England, Their England* is all about the consequences of that war. Its frequent comparisons between battle and cricket are of a stock kind and entirely jocular, but when, in a following chapter, Donald visits the Vale of Aylesbury, the mock-pastoral of the Invalids' visit to Fordenden modulates into the actual social history of post-war rural England. Wandering into a local pub, Donald gets talking with a group of elderly locals. The conversation keeps returning to 'the War', which, as one of them remarks, 'put a stop to a great many things'. The community has lost a whole generation of young men, 42 from the village having been killed. Donald ventures a remark about national honour to which one of the ageing men asks, 'what national honour does for me?' He had three sons and eight grandsons fighting for national honour. Three were killed, two lost legs, the village has lost its young men and those they died for are worse off than before. And there's a shortage of cricketers.

The interweaving of history, war, rural England and cricket becomes explicit in the visionary final chapter of the novel, 'The Peaceful Green Fields of England'. Donald is visiting Winchester, 'city of Alfred, once capital of England'. He wanders through the Cathedral, full of memorials to long-dead English soldiers, and out into the graveyard where those who have died more recently in Flanders, France and the Dardanelles are buried, and into the grounds of its famous college, older even than Eton. He stretches out on a grassy slope, 'like a deck-chair', and looks down on the 'glittering streams of the Itchen' to the 'white tiny dots of cricketers' in the College playing fields, 'the click of cricket-ball on cricket bat' mingling with 'the tinkling of sheep-bells across the vales of the chalkland'. These closing pages of the novel, all trace of its earlier satire and absurdist comedy now gone, offer an idealised picture of England's past in which cricket becomes part of a soundtrack celebrating the once 'green and kindly land of England'. The novel closes to 'the muted voices of grazing sheep, and the merry click of bat upon ball [...] and the bells of the Cathedral'. The world, for a moment, stands still, but the persistence of scenes such as this in a post-war world is uncertain.

The sounds of cricket echo through the fiction of this period, audible even in such an unlikely novel as Virginia Woolf's *Mrs Dalloway* (1925). This opens with Clarissa Dalloway out walking in central London on a fresh June morning: 'The war was over', she thinks, 'thank Heaven – over [...] everywhere [...] there was a beating, a stirring of galloping ponies, tapping of cricket bats; Lords, Ascot'. We're in the metropolis, not rural England, but the scene is described as a kind of urban pastoral in which the sound of bat on ball celebrates the end of the disturbance and suffering wrought by war and the restoration of traditional life. In this manner, Woolf's novel occupies similar ground to the village cricket fiction of that period. Later in the novel, however, cricket will be shown as providing no comfort to the persisting and tragic consequences of that conflict.

England, Their England ends nostalgically while also questioning nostalgia. Hugh De Sélincourt's classic work of cricket fiction between the wars, *The Cricket Match* (1924), is similarly poised between past and present. Its setting is the Sussex village of Tillingford, nestling in a hollow under the Downs. The novel is confined to the events of one day, its 15-hour time span so beautifully proportioned that it seems almost to unfold in real time. It opens with a description of the village at dawn on 4 August 1921, the day of Tillingford's annual fixture with their old rivals, the neighbouring village of Raveley. The sun's rays are breaking through the 'gentle encircling haze […] the mill pond [is] beginning to gleam in the early morning light', smoke is rising from the cottages and slowly dispersing in the still air. We're in another pastoral scene but without the satiric exaggeration of Macdonell's description.

From the opening page however, notes of unease disturb the placid timelessness of the setting. The acres of tall fir trees which until recently surrounded the village have been felled by a keen businessman, a war profiteer who'd used German prisoners to level the trees to be sawn into pit props for the mining industry. Bungalows are springing up around the edges of the village. The cricket ground itself is under threat. It has a bad dip to one side that needs filling but money for this has not been forthcoming from the Parish Council. Home to the football club in winter, the turf is being worn thinner and thinner by the year and is desperately in need of a fallow season to be properly dressed and sown. The cricket club has managed only a 'staggering recovery since the war' and there is a spreading feeling of 'melancholy certainty that each season must surely be the last'.

Set against this, however, is the dedication of its members and, in particular, the figure of Horace Cairie, aged 15, the first of a succession of young cricketers we meet in the opening chapters of cricket novels as they wake, breakfast and prepare to face the day. Horace is up at quarter past five, his mind full of the match even though he's not sure yet if he'll be playing. He pulls back the curtains. It's a perfect day for cricket, and there's still time for him to be asked to play, which later that morning, after someone withdraws, he is. This foundational scene of village cricket fiction is intrinsic to cricket itself, a game almost uniquely dependent on the vagaries of the weather. Joe Root has recently recalled: 'When I was 12,

I would wake up in the morning and open the curtains and pray it wasn't raining so I could play.'

Most cricket fiction of this era, whether set on a village green, the grounds of a wealthy landowner's estate or the playing fields of a public school, features a 'young un' who pulls it off and wins the day. That afternoon, coming in at number 11, Horace will have a last wicket partnership of 22 with John McLeod, aged 50, the oldest member of the team, which will prove just enough to take the home side to a winning total. And after tea, when Tillingford takes the field, Horace makes a diving catch at a crucial moment which helps secure victory for his team. His agility in the field reminds Mr Hodgkiss, an 'old, old man' watching from his favourite seat in front of the pavilion – another recurring figure in cricket fiction of this time – of when he too had been 'a keen little nipper […] winning his spurs'. No one left in the village now remembers the old man's former prowess, but the 'young un' implies that cricket in the village will, somehow, persist. Later in the novel, as if to confirm this, we're given a future glimpse of him as an adult cricketer perpetuating all that is still best in the spirit of the game.

But the match itself is only part of the story and perhaps not the main part, occupying as it does only the second half of the novel. The early chapters take us slowly around the village, introducing some of the team who will figure that afternoon. There's Sid Smith, a labourer, at home in a cramped cottage with his wife and three young kids, lighting a Woodbine and searching for his cricket trousers, which he finds have been shat on by the baby, breakfasting on a couple of slices of bread and dripping before setting off on a three-mile walk to the bricklayer's yard to put in a morning's work before the match. In sharp contrast, Edgar Trine, son of the manor, has a morning tea-tray delivered to his bed by the housemaid who then sorts through his clothes to pick out a pair of flannels from the five he has to choose from. Trine complains about their poor quality: 'Such foul flannel […] since the war'.

Around the village, we're taken. John McLeod, the mainstay of the club, is unwrapping a parcel of sky-blue cricket caps that he's ordered and, like a county captain, will distribute among the team that morning. Tom Hunter is in his bicycle shop mending a puncture and complaining about how news of him needing to have his teeth replaced has spread around the village. Tom was gassed and suffered trench fever in the War, and his temper is not what it was. Sam Bird, the 'ceremonious' umpire 'who somehow gave importance to everything he did', is irritated by the lads of the village kicking a football around as he puts in the wickets and blames their unruliness on their fathers having been away at the war.

And so on. In a series of vignettes, De Sélincourt sketches the character of the village, its social structure, its habits and customs and how it is coming to terms with the disturbances brought by the First World War. Class differences are sketched with humour and a light touch but also a clear-sighted view of how they define the village. Edgar Trine's mother is delighted her son is playing for the village: 'With all this discontent that's about nowadays, it is so good for them all', to which Trine laughingly replies: 'Mater [...] You're becoming a regular Bolshie.' Other passing references to Bolshevism keep us in mind of the recent Russian Revolution.

Mrs Trine's faith in cricket as a solvent of class differences is not entirely true even of the match itself. Trine and Henry Waite, a smart young gentleman down from London, drift naturally together as the team assembles. John McLeod, who opens the innings with Waite, resents the supercilious manner of his partner, a feeling intensified by Waite's condescending courtesy after several misunderstandings in running between the wickets. The elderly Tillingford scorer describes Waite's manner as 'His rank and stink'. When another flustered call results in Waite being run-out, McLeod's resentment is compounded by humiliation and guilt.

Such tensions are briefly forgotten in the excitement and aftermath of victory. At the start of the afternoon, Sid Smith had looked enviously at the cut of Trine's flannels, but when Trine takes the winning catch off his bowling, the social gulf between the two men disappears: 'They were just two men in flannels'. Yet on Monday evening, when they pass each other in the village, Sid gives Trine a 'rather surly salute', which the other resents: 'Damn it he thinks [...] I don't despise him for being a working man'! Class reconciliation, such as it had been the previous afternoon, spreads no further than the cricket field.

For the moment, however, harmony reigns. The team captain, riding home on his bicycle, admires the red and orange glow of the sky, the stillness of the evening, its glory. The sound of a band playing in the village square carries up into the surrounding hills. Several of the team have drifted off to the pub. Sid reaches home and with relief takes off his boots. And young Horace has made his father come out onto the lawn and bowl to him.

The founding story of the village cricket tradition, its incunabula, is Mary Russell Mitford's 'A Country Cricket Match', first published in the July 1823 issue of the *Lady's Magazine*. Mitford established the setting, the atmosphere, the conventions and many of the character types which subsequent writers of the village cricket story would use. The opening paragraph of her story also gives an overview of the types of cricket played at that time and anticipates Orwell in capturing why village cricket is above all other forms of the game, 'the thing'. For these reasons, as well as the brio of her writing, I shall quote from that paragraph at length.

I doubt if there be any scene in the world more animating or delightful than a cricket match; – I do not mean a set match at Lord's Ground for money, hard money; between a certain number of gentlemen and players, as they are called – people who make a trade of that noble sport, and degrade it into an affair of bettings and hedgings and cheatings [...] like boxing or horse-racing: nor do I mean a pretty fete in a gentleman's park, where one club of cricketing dandies encounters another such club, and where they show off in graceful costume to a gay marquee of admiring belles, who condescend so to purchase admiration, and while away a long summer morning in partaking of cold collations, conversing occasionally, and seeming to understand the game; – the whole being conducted according to ballroom etiquette, so as to be exceedingly elegant and exceedingly dull. No! the cricket that I mean is a real solid, old-fashioned match between neighbouring parishes, where each attacks the other for honour and a supper, glory, and half-a-crown a man. If there be any gentleman amongst them, it is well – if not, it is so much the better. Your gentleman cricketer is in general rather an anomalous character. Elderly gentlemen are obviously good for nothing; and young beaux are, for the most part, hampered and trammelled by dress and habit; the stiff cravat, the pinched in waist, the dandy walk – oh, they will never do for cricket! Now, our country lads, accustomed to the flail or the hammer (your blacksmiths are capital hitters), have the free use of their arms; they know how to move their shoulders; and they can move their feet too – they can run [...] No! a village match is the thing – where our highest officer – our conductor [...] is but a little farmer's second son; where a day-labourer is our bowler, and a blacksmith our long-stop; where the spectators consist of retired cricketers, the veterans of the green, the careful mothers, the girls, and all the boys of two parishes […] where laughing and shouting, and the very ecstasy of merriment and good humour, prevail.

Mitford was the precocious child of a spendthrift father. At the age of 10, she boosted her father's gambling and lavish spending by drawing him a £20,000 prize in the Irish Lottery, having chosen the number 2224 because the digits made up the sum of her age. But her father's extravagance ruined the family, and in 1820 they were forced to move from their estate in Reading to a labourer's cottage in the village of Three Mile Cross, a few miles south of the town. Mitford had already been helping to support her family through writing poetry and plays, but the collapse of their finances forced her to turn, as she puts it, 'from the lofty steep of tragic poetry to the every-day path of village stories'. 'A Country Cricket Match' was one of the earliest of these stories and sketches, which were collected in a series of five volumes between 1824 and 1832 under the title *Our Village*. They saved the family from penury and made her famous. She remained in Three Mile Cross for over thirty years until moving to the nearby village of Swallowfield, where she died in 1855 after a carriage accident.

The defining element of Mitford's story, one which is almost constant in the tradition of village cricket writing, is the social feeling and personal pride, as she puts it, in 'belonging to a parish, breathing the same air, looking on the same trees, listening to the same nightingales', the parochial patriotism in being able to speak of 'our side'. But this doesn't, of course, prevent complications and ill-feeling in selecting the team: resentment over the preference of one player to another, a late withdrawal or one of the eleven failing to turn up, features still familiar to anyone captaining a small local club. Mitford treats these petty ructions with humour and in doing so provides character sketches of most of the team, their strengths and weaknesses, their social positions, their ages and their occupations. There are two blacksmiths and the last-minute inclusion of a 'young un', recurring figures and tropes in subsequent village cricket writing.

Mitford apologises for not leaving herself space for 'the details of our victory', but this is also true of many subsequent village cricket stories where the build-up to the match is often as significant and involving as the game itself. In the event, Mitford's match is a one-sided affair, with none of the last-ball drama that was to become the hallmark of later cricket fiction. The visiting 'men of B' make only 22, 'our team' replies with 169, after which the visitors refuse to bat a second time. But the pages she does give to the cricket are full of period detail. Runs are 'notches', in those days the method of scoring. The outfield is 'wretched [...] the ball would not run a yard', and lob bowling is a favoured and highly effective style.

Mitford's story also has elements of realism often absent in those which followed. Her 'young-un', a 'pretty boy', the last-minute inclusion who in later stories will save the day, is 'seized with such a fit of shame-faced shyness that he could scarcely hold his bat' and is bowled first ball without attempting a shot. And it rains. How it rains. On the morning of the match 'the sky promised a series of deluging showers, and kept its word'. There are soaking showers throughout the day and by the end the players are 'all wet through [but] all good humoured, and all happy – except the losers'. It is the rain that causes the mishaps which no later story will be without. The home team's long-stop falls sprawling in the mud, and a sudden rush of cricketers from the field to escape another pelting shower tips over a group of spectators sitting on an unstable bench and sends them flying into a ditch. As Mitford concludes: 'Who would think that a little bit of leather, and two pieces of wood, had such a delightful and delighting power.'

Dingley Dell versus All-Muggleton, the cricket match in Charles Dickens' *The Pickwick Papers* (1837), is more celebrated than Mitford's story, but the only thing it really offered to the later tradition of village cricket writing was its pastoral opening and its riotous aftermath. Mr Pickwick wakes on the morning of the match to a perfect country scene:

> The rich, sweet smell of the hayricks rose to his chamber window; the hundred perfumes of the little flower-garden beneath scented the air around; the deep-green meadows shone in the morning dew that glistened on every leaf as it trembled in the gentle air; and the birds sang as if every sparkling drop were a fountain of inspiration to them.

It is a morning of similar promise to those that the protagonists of future village cricket stories will awaken to, but Mr Pickwick has no idea that he will be involved in a cricket match and in truth he hardly is. Arriving at the All-Muggleton ground, he is shown into a marquee – this is a more socially elevated fixture than Mitford's – where they 'notch', and there he remains. He plays no part in the match itself in which, indeed, only four players are ever named – Mr Dumkins and Mr Podder for the All-Muggletons and Mr Luffey and Mr Struggles for Dingley Dell, the stars of their respective team. Mr Pickwick watches from the safe distance of the marquee as each fielder 'fixed himself into the proper attitude by placing one hand on each knee, and stooping very much as if he were "making a back" for some beginner at leap-frog'. Mr Dumkins hits the first ball of the match over the heads of several fielders 'who had just stooped low enough to let it fly over them'.

And that's pretty much it, apart from the verbose Mr Jingle's description of a single-wicket contest he'd once played in the West Indies, probably the first appearance in fiction of cricket in a colonial setting. As for the match itself, All-Muggleton notches 54, a total well beyond the efforts of the Dingley Dellers, and the teams adjourn to the Blue Lion Inn where at midnight they can still be heard singing 'with great feeling and emphasis, the beautiful and pathetic national air of "We won't go home 'till morning [repeated three times] Till daylight doth appear"'.

Dickens himself described cricket as 'the social cement of the classes' and asked, rhetorically, if there was 'any week in England, or in the world, like the Canterbury Week'. Two years before his death, in 1868, he became chair of his local Gad's Hill Cricket Club and advised its team captain, his son Harry, that gentlemen should pay twice the sub of its working-class members but that everyone should have an equal vote.

Another forerunner of the village cricket story that was to reach its apogee in the 1920s and 1930s is H. G. Wells' 'The Veteran Cricketer' (1894), about an old cricketer who 'earns a precarious livelihood, and certainly the sincere aversion of the countryside, by umpiring'. Strictly speaking, this is not a work of fiction but a fictionalised picture of Wells' father, Joseph, who, playing for Kent against Sussex in 1862, became the first bowler in a first-class match to take four wickets in four balls (the second of his victims was Jane Austen's great-nephew). But it is as much fiction as memoir and offers a delightful bridge between Mitford and De Sélincourt's worlds of village cricket.

As a lad, Joseph Wells worked as an under-gardener on an estate adjacent to the stately home of Penshurst Place and across the road from where the Duke family, to whom Joseph was related, made their already famous cricket balls. He married Sarah Neale, a maid at another great house in the area, and the couple bought a small and grindingly unsuccessful crockery shop in Bromley High Street where they also sold cricket goods provided by the Dukes. It was here that H. G. was born. Joseph revived the Bromley Cricket Club, played for the West Kent club throughout the 1860s and supplemented his meagre earnings from the shop by hiring himself out to wealthy landed families in the area for matches against their surrounding gentry neighbours, more profitable work than the paltry match fees paid to county cricketers at the time. His playing days were ended by a fall from a ladder which left him permanently lame, an accident said by his son to have occurred while pruning a grapevine in his small back garden, but rumoured in the town to have happened when helping a lady friend escape over the back wall after Sarah had returned unexpectedly early from church. H. G. was no cricketer but in other ways very much his father's son. Joseph's playing days over, he turned to umpiring to eke out some extra money, officiating at both public school and village fixtures around West Kent.

The umpire in 'The Veteran Cricketer' is earning a few shillings and a pint or two at a village game. His method is peremptory and pedagogic: 'Out, Billy Durgan, and one you ought to ha' hit for four'. He has a particular distaste for the local vicar: 'Respect he shows by a punctilious touching of his hat brim, directed to the sacred office; all the rest is malignity, and aimed at the man that fills it.' The vicar, a characteristically inept figure in village cricket stories, is well-meaning, earnest and nervous, 'a tall lean man of ascetic visage and ample garments, a soul clothed not so much in a fleshy body as in black flaps'. On his coming to the wicket, the umpire brusquely corrects the vicar's stance, rebukes him for not playing with a straight bat, ignores his ingratiating questions about the health of the umpire's chickens, and, while 'touching his hat at intervals', continues to comment disparagingly on the vicar's batting while the field 'sniggers none too furtively'. Very soon the humiliated vicar gets himself out, dismissed on all fronts. It was often said that cricket was the Church of England at play, but Joseph Wells would have none of it.

The tone softens and broadens as we hear the 'ancient cricketer' recalling the throwing controversy when overarm bowling began and deploring 'your modern billiard-table pitch', much preferring 'a cunning obliquity in a wicket that would send the balls mysteriously askew'. Nostalgia slowly takes over as we hear of an earlier time of 'stone jars with cool drink swishing therein [...] of eleven men in a drag (a horse-drawn coach), and tuneful and altogether glorious home-comings by the light of the moon', their voices echoing like those in the Blue Lion Inn. The story closes with a contrast between the glory days when every village was a 'home and nursery of stalwart cricketers' and the present epoch of 'special trains, gate-money, star elevens, and the tumultuous gathering of idle cads to jabber at a game they cannot play'.

There are many clear lines of continuity between nineteenth-century renderings of the village cricket story and its twentieth-century versions. De Sélincourt's *The Village Cricket Match* is a kind of homage to Mitford's story, and in *England, Their England* Macdonell develops and amplifies the comic potential already apparent in the genre. Siegfried Sassoon's 'The Flower Show Match', an early chapter of his fictionalised autobiography *Memoirs of a Fox-Hunting Man* (1928), is an *entre deux guerres* village cricket story with debts to both Mitford and Sassoon's contemporaries.

Apart from a prelude in which the young narrator, George Sherston, arrives home from his public school and learns to his excitement that he will be playing in the flower show match the next day, the story is, like De Sélincourt's novel, confined to a single day. Once again we have the 'young-un' waking early and relishing the promise of a 'flushed and brightening sky', although in social position he's much closer to Edgar Trine than to Horace Cairie. We see Dixon, the all-competent retainer of the Sherston house, cleaning his boots for him.

The day follows a similar pattern to De Sélincourt's novel. We walk with our young protagonist to the ground, meet several of the home team, Butley, and see the visitors, Rotherden, arrive. The year is 1903 and the Butley team is dressed in a manner that would seem 'unorthodox […] to modern eyes': one of them wears a pale-pink shirt and grey trousers, another dingy white trousers with thin green stripes. George, however, wears a black and yellow scarf around his waist, showing that he's won a place in his House eleven.

Rotherden has come fourteen miles in a two-horse brake, and there's no hurry to get the match started. When finally it does, the first ball, as in *England, Their England,* is described in particular detail.

Peckham is a fast bowler with an eccentric style. Like most fast bowlers, he starts about fifteen paces from the wicket, but instead of *running* he *walks* the whole way to the crease, very much on his heels, breaking his aggressive stride with a couple of systematic hops when about half-way to his destination. Now he is ready. Seamark (the umpire) pronounces the word 'Play!' and off he goes, walking for all he is worth, gripping the ball ferociously, and eying the batsman as if he intended to murder him if he can't bowl him neck and crop. On the ultimate stride his arm swings over, and a short-pitched ball pops up and whizzes alarmingly near Crump's magnificent moustache.

I've quoted this in full because it's such a remarkable anticipation of Jasprit Bumrah's run-up and delivery.

The match itself is described in much less detail than in Macdonell or De Sélincourt, and although George hits the winning run, there is none of the climax of the tie at Fordenden or the victory at Tillingford. It is cricket as the centrepiece of a wider community occasion that most interests Sassoon. The ground is ringed with tents – the Horticultural Tent, the Luncheon Tent, the Tea Tent and the Beer Tent. There are swings, roundabouts and a brass band. This is an Edwardian village festival with all the trimmings yet with odd notes of discord as well. One of these, when the band while playing 'The Soldiers of the Queen' is overwhelmed by a steam-organ bursting into 'a strident and blaring fanfaronade' as it accompanies the roundabout, is comic. Less amusing for the village is that the winner of the best vegetable competition is discovered to have purchased his prize-winning entry in a neighbouring village, which certainly isn't playing the game. One might also wonder if Butley's one-legged and 'grossly partisan' umpire, Bill Sutler, is really playing the game when, as it's suggested, he uses his wooden leg to make dents in the pitch to assist the home team's bowlers.

As with De Sélincourt and Macdonell, the main difference between Sassoon's story and its nineteenth-century prototypes is the intrusion of the world beyond the village into the placid parochial scene. Once again war adds a sombre background to the cricket and to village life. This time it's the so-called Boer War, more accurately the South African War, which is being fought as they play. The village grocer's calendar hanging from a nail in the pantry of George's home has a picture of 'The Relief of Ladysmith', one of those triumphant disasters of which British military history is so proud. One of the Butley team is recently returned from serving on the veldt. At lunch he's toasted by the players of both sides, and when he goes out to bat later in the afternoon he's given 'a Boer War ovation', although as he confides to George, he never actually set eyes on a Boer the whole time he was in South Africa. Other wars hover in the background. Village tradition has it that the Butley umpire lost his leg while fighting for

Queen and Country, and sitting outside the Tea Tent enjoying the afternoon spree is a very old woman, Miss Clara Maskell, stone-deaf for more than sixty years, born in the year of the Battle of Waterloo.

War then provides a dark as well as patriotic background music to the cricket in these novels. Or perhaps it is the sound of cricket itself which is the requiem. This is particularly so of L. P. Hartley's *The Go-Between* (1953), a later novel but a retrospective one which looks back to the same period as Sassoon's, the beginning of a century that opened 'winged with hope' but has proved to be 'the most changeful half a century in history'. The narrator, Leo Colston, is remembering the long hot summer of 1900 when, aged 13, he spent his school vacation in Norfolk at Brandham Hall, the stately home of a socially superior school friend, Marcus. The Boer War is in progress and frequently mentioned. Leo had 'gone almost mad with excitement at the relief of Ladysmith' earlier that year, and enjoys singing 'The Soldiers of the Queen'. Boer War generals feature in the games Leo and Marcus play in the grounds of the house.

More vividly, Lord Trimingham, whose family were the historic owners of Brandham Hall, has been injured in the fighting, his face carrying a 'sickle-shaped scar that ran from his eye to the corner of his mouth [...] [and] pulled the eye down, exposing a tract of glistening red underlid, and the mouth up, so that you could see the gums above his teeth'. Trimingham is a guest at Brandham Hall, and an engagement between him and Marcus's sister Marian is expected to be announced. Marian, however, is having an affair with Ted Burgess, a local tenant farmer, and Leo – the go-between – has been recruited to carry messages between the surreptitious lovers.

The cricket match in Hartley's novel mirrors its plot, with Trimingham captaining the Hall and Burgess the village. It's an annual affair which, as Marcus explains to Leo, putting it more bluntly than Edgar Trine's mother, 'helps to keep them quiet'. Hartley knows his cricket. Trimingham's late cut is said to rival R. E. Foster's and Ted Burgess is described as a 'village Jessop'. Foster was on a roll in 1900, scoring centuries for Oxford in the annual university match and in both innings for the Gentlemen against the Players. In July of that year, the same month as the match at Brandham Hall, Jessop scored pre-lunch centuries in both innings of a county match for Gloucester against Yorkshire. Two years later he was to hit one of the most famous of all test centuries, 104 in 77 minutes against the Australians at the Oval. Many of his 17 fours in that innings would have been sixes except that in those days a six had to be hit out of the ground. One of his boundaries was caught on the players' balcony.

Leo remembers how on the day of the match, class distinctions within the Hall team were forgotten – 'the butler, the footman, the coachman, the gardener and the pantry-boy seemed completely on an equality with us' – but this brief moment of levelling up doesn't extend to the opposition. Whereas the Hall players are all correctly dressed in white flannels, some of the villagers have turned out in their working clothes and braces. Leo sees this contrast as being like 'trained soldiers fighting natives', but then wonders if perhaps the village team isn't more like the Boers, 'who did not have much in the way of equipment by our standards, but could give a good account of themselves, none the less'. Parallels between the match and the current war in South Africa continue. As the Hall loses wickets, Leo describes the villagers celebrating like 'Boers in their motley raiment, triumphantly throwing the ball into the air after each kill'. He imagines the locals dotted around the boundary to be 'animated by a revolutionary spirit, and revelling in the downfall of their betters'.

When the village team bats, Ted Burgess lives up to his description as a 'village Jessop'. A flurry of fours is followed by a 'glorious six which sailed over the pavilion and dropped among the trees at the back', the equivalent of Jessop hitting the gasometer at the Oval. 'Dimly', as Leo recalls, he perceived the match had become even more than a conflict between the Hall and the village. It was also a 'struggle [...] between obedience to tradition and defiance of it, between social stability and revolution'.

All the while, Leo has been watching from the pavilion. In a slight variation on the 'young-un' narrative, he is twelfth man for the Hall, not a late inclusion. But an injury to the long-on fielder as he tries to catch one of Burgess's cannonball drives brings Leo onto the field where he nervously takes up his position at square leg. We're down to the last over, the ninth wicket has just fallen, eight runs are needed for victory and Trimingham is bowling to Burgess. Hartley had certainly read a few cricket stories. But in *The Go-Between*, so much more is at stake than the familiar drama of bowler and batter: there's 'tenant and landlord, commoner and peer, village and Hall', and Marian, sitting on the pavilion steps, watching her intended bowl to her lover. Love and cricket are simultaneously at issue.

The end of the match is entirely conventional. Burgess clouts Trimingham to leg, Leo throws up his arm above his head, and the ball sticks in his palm. The Hall has won. But the numbing pain Leo feels in his hand is intensified and complicated by a 'pang of regret, sharp as a sword thrust'. He adores Marian, likes Burgess, admires Trimingham – whose side is he on? Victory for one side, defeat for the other, is far too simple for the entangled world of love, class and nation in which he's caught.

At the novel's end, Leo, aged 65, returns to the village and visits Marian, now the elderly widowed Lady Trimingham living alone in a small house that once belonged to her nanny. He learns from her that Burgess had subsequently committed suicide, Trimingham is long dead, Marcus and his older brother were killed in the First World War, as were her son and his wife in the Second. It is 1952. The Korean War is in progress. Britain has just exploded its first atom bomb.

As Leo revisits the scenes of that long hot summer of 1900, he stands in the churchyard from where he can look down on the cricket field.

> It was mid-May, and they had been mowing it and rolling and generally putting it in order for the season. Evidently cricket still flourished in Brandham. The pavilion was still there, facing me, and I tried to make out where I had been standing when I made my historic catch, wondering what it felt like to be a cricketer, for cricket was another thing I had been excused when I went back to school.

Leo, as befits a go-between, stands there poised between past and present. He never played cricket again after that summer; this young-un was not to have a proleptic role. But somehow the game itself has persisted through a half-century described by Marian as 'hideous […] which has denatured humanity and planted death and hate where love and living were'. The world hasn't stood still, but some things, cricket for example, have survived, no matter how sadly or nostalgically.

E. M. Forster stipulated that because of its homosexual theme his novel *Maurice*, written in 1914, should not be published in his lifetime. It was eventually published in 1971, a year after his death. The cricket match in the novel has a similar setting to *The Go-Between* but to a very different purpose. Its 'action date', as Forster put it, 'is about 1912', and the house and estate of Penge, 'marked […] with the immobility that precedes decay', suggests Brandham Hall, but there's no hint of war, and the description of the cricket is, to say the least, cursory. But the match is nevertheless of defining significance, functioning in a similar manner to Hartley's to mirror and dramatise its central theme.

There is no build-up of excited anticipation to the cricket in Forster's novel. Clive, the owner of Penge, describes the fixture as 'that awful Park v. Village cricket match', and his friend, Maurice, the main protagonist, who is visiting for the occasion, hates the game. On the night before the match, the gamekeeper of the estate, Alec Scudder, climbs up a ladder into Maurice's room, and they spend the night together. The next morning, Alec has to leave early because he's needed to roll the cricket pitch. Forster's tone in this novel is often unsteady, but here I assume it is deliberately playful.

The match itself is the most casually rendered of any I've described since Dingley Dell versus All-Muggleton. On hearing that the Park has won the toss, Maurice doesn't bother to go down to the ground for the first half hour. There's a nod to convention – the vicar is bowling lobs – but we never learn the score nor the names of the players apart from Alec, Maurice and the donkey-dropping vicar, Mr Borenius. Alec is the Park's most competent cricketer and its captain. When Maurice comes in to join him, their eyes meet, Alec smiles and begins to attack the bowling:

> Maurice played up too [...] he felt they were against the whole world, that not only Mr Borenius and the field but the audience in the shed and all England were closing round the wickets. They played for the sake of each other and of their fragile relationship – if one fell the other would follow. They intended no harm to the world, but so long as it attacked they must punish, they must stand wary, then hit with full strength, they must show that when two are gathered together majorities shall not triumph. And as the game proceeded it connected with the night, and interpreted it.

But when Clive belatedly arrives at the ground, Alec departs the field: 'It was only fit and proper that the squire should bat at once.' As Alec goes, Maurice follows, giving up his wicket as an expression of his feelings for Alec.

Unlike *The Go-Between*, *Maurice* will end happily as Forster had declared it must: 'I was determined that in fiction anyway two men should fall in love and remain in it for the ever and ever that fiction allows.' And so, also unlike *The Go-Between*, this cricket match is a place of social defiance and fulfilled desire, of oneness against the world, rather than a scene of battle between two men competing over a woman. Forster's cricket match is both an expression of, and cover for, so much else.

Both *Maurice* and *The Go-Between* have interesting connections with D. H. Lawrence's *Lady Chatterley's Lover* (1928). Although Alec pre-dates D. H. Lawrence's gamekeeper, Mellors, they are associated through cricket. There are three distinct versions of *Lady Chatterley's Lover*, and in the second, *John Thomas and Lady Jane*, the gamekeeper's father (like H. G. Wells's) is a professional cricketer. The influence of Lawrence's novel on *The Go-Between* is patent, not just in terms of the transgressive class nature of the central love relationship of both novels, Ted Burgess and Marian being versions of Mellors and Connie Chatterley, but also in the war wounds that both Lord Tringingham and Sir Clifford Chatterley carry. Chatterley has come back from the First World War 'more or less in bits', paralysed from the waist down, and Tringingham is badly scarred. The class they represent is visibly in decline; the class that Alec, Mellors (called Parkin in *John Thomas and Lady Lane*) and Burgess embody is vital, alive and sexually potent.

For the first half of the twentieth century, village cricket offered a significant setting for serious literary fiction. Quite apart from the example of a pre-eminent novelist such as Forster, Sassoon's *Memoirs of a Fox-Hunting Man* and Macdonell's *England, Their England* both won the James Tait Black Memorial Prize for fiction, and *The Go-Between* was joint winner of the Heinemann Award (a prize for non-fiction and poetry as well as novels). Each of these writers of fiction understood that cricket, apart from its intrinsic fascination, had the potential for exploring and dramatising many other things as well: war and its aftermath; class difference and antagonism; sex and morality, for example. And underlying these themes is the question of England itself, its culture, its identity, its past, present and future.

Which raises the question, what has become of the village cricket story? Why has it disappeared as a form of literary fiction in which cricket is an optic or a trigger for other things besides? Can it no longer stand for England in the way that it did for those early and mid-twentieth-century novelists? Is its only remaining purpose to capture and express nostalgia?

John Parker's *The Village Cricket Match* (1977), a 'replay' as he describes it, of De Sélincourt's *The Cricket Match*, suggests the latter. It opens neatly with the description of a simple granite cross in a corner of the Tillingford ground, a memorial to the dead of two world wars, but immediately spoils this with a laboured account of how the County Archives in Chichester would uncover the names of many others from the village who fought with Wellington in Spain and Harry at Agincourt. His attempt to show us the world of De Sélincourt's novel 50 years on is similarly leaden. The altered social landscape and demography of the contemporary world is delivered as a series of short lectures rather than as part of the dramatic texture of the novel. We're informed: 'Inevitably, Tillingfold had grown somewhat in the past twenty years'. We learn that Raveley, the opposing team, is no longer a village but a town of more than 100,000 and those 'monuments to modern culture – Woolworths, Littlewoods, Marks and Spencer [...]' (the list goes on) have taken over the old village street. The social composition of its team is different from Tillingfold's, including a Pakistani, a South African, an Australian and a Jamaican, but in Parker's hands, they're flat ethnic stereotypes. There's far too much telling and not enough showing, except that is when we come to the match itself, a near ball-by-ball account running to almost 100 pages, two-thirds of the whole novel, very different from the elegant proportioning and manner of De Sélincourt's story. Parker's replay becomes a mere run-chase. Even re-enactment should bring something new to the table.

Horace Ove's 1986 film *Playing Away*, with a screenplay by Caryl Phillips published in book form the following year, does just that. Phillips was born on the Caribbean island of St Kitts, grew up in Leeds, studied at Oxford and is now Professor of English at Yale. He is also, coincidentally, another winner of the James Tait prize for his novel *Crossing the River* (1993).

Playing Away involves the visit of an ethnic Caribbean cricket team from Brixton to the rural Suffolk village of Sneddington. The match is to be the climax of Sneddington's 'Third World Week'. In shape and treatment it has much in common with De Sélincourt and Macdonell's stories, though it is spread over a weekend rather than contained within a single day. Like the Invalids team in *England, Their England*, the Brixton Conquistadors are slow to assemble, get lost on the way and arrive late. And like *The Cricket Match*, the early scenes offer glimpses of the inner lives of several characters from both teams. Willie Boy, captain of the Brixton side, is wrestling with whether or not to return to Jamaica, the home he left many years ago. Playing away has several layers of meaning for him. Derek, the captain of Sneddington, a City banker, spends all his leisure time at the village pub or on the cricket field. His neglected wife, Viv, when asked by Jeff, one of the visitors, in a tender late-night scene if she cares for her husband, replies: 'Have you ever watched a candle go out?' These snapshots of the troubled lives of characters from both teams give personal depth to pre-match episodes such as the vicar's tea-party in which the cultural differences between the two teams are exploited for comedy, and other scenes which dramatise tensions within as well as between the sides.

The match itself is both generic and genre-breaking. The Conquistadores are a man short, but the ring-in is one of the women who's come with the team, Maisie, and it's she, not a young-un, who takes a game-changing catch in the outfield. The home umpire, Godfrey, is blatantly one-sided, but his decisions are all in favour of the visitors with whom he has a quiet sympathy. This provokes Ian, one of several disaffected youths in the village who sit outside the local looking bored, into leading a walk-off by half the village team when yet another decision goes against his bowling. Only Derek, a couple of his posh friends and the vicar are left on the field. The class differences which were smoothed over or temporarily reconciled in earlier stories of village cricket, here break out on the field and result in Sneddington losing the game. Social deference has vanished, and so too has that team spirit which Donald Cameron had gone looking for half a century earlier.

So where does this leave the village cricket-writing tradition? The comedy of *Playing Away* is as fresh as ever. Cricket remains a sport of unique potential for mishap, the unlikely and cutting down to size the pretensions of its participants. But in a world of cultural and ethnic differences, the unhurried informality of playing away has been lost. When Willie Boy asks if there will be 'a tea break or something', he's curtly told, 'Straight around'. And as the Conquistadores pile back into their coach, he complains that they haven't even been offered an after-match drink. Sneddington has lost; the visitors have been snubbed; this won't become an annual fixture. And the village team is falling apart. Rather than assuaging class resentments, the village cricket match has brought them to a head, disrupting the game and leaving only five men – the banker, a couple of his posh mates (described by another of the team as 'stuck up little twats') and that remnant of the past – the vicar – facing a team of black cricketers from Brixton as the evening shadow of the local church spreads across the grass. You can almost hear the knell of parting day. *Playing Away* seems like the end point, a recessional for the tradition I've been tracing. Cricket writing in fiction must now look elsewhere. But in drawing the curtain on this kind of writing, Ove and Phillips also suggested other places it might look.

Chapter 2

THE PUBLIC SCHOOL CRICKET STORY

There's a breathless hush in the close tonight –
Ten to make and the match to win –
A bumping pitch and a blinding light,
An hour to play and the last man in.
And it's not for the sake of a ribboned coat,
Or the selfish hope of a season's fame,
But his Captain's hand on his shoulder smote –
'Play up! play up! and play the game!'

The sand of the desert is sodden red, -
Red with the wreck of a square that broke; -
The Gatling's jammed and the Colonel dead,
And the regiment blind with dust and smoke.
The river of death has brimmed his banks,
And England's far, and Honour a name,
But the voice of a schoolboy rallies the ranks;
'Play up! play up! and play the game!'

– Henry Newbolt, 'Vitai Lampada'

My head is full of the ghosts of men in white playing games before
the Great War.

– Hilary Mantel

If the village green was one favourite setting for the cricket story in fiction,
the public school was the other, and it was from these two very different
sources that the association of cricket with Englishness flowed. Test and
county cricket figure very little in fiction, one reason being that the contained settings of the village and public school function more readily as
versions of the nation at large than other forms of the game. Common to
both is a feeling of being the member of a community.

The earliest example of the public school cricket story, Thomas Hughes' *Tom Brown's Schooldays* (1857) has some features more reminiscent of Mitford and Dickens than the novels of the later public school tradition. The climax of Hughes's novel is Rugby's great event of the cricketing year, the match against Marylebone, the 'delight of the town and the neighbourhood' as well as the school. The Lord's men arrive by train the afternoon before, 'hard-bitten, wiry, whiskered fellows', illustrious and intimidating cricketers who leave the school team feeling despondent about its chances the next day. But this mood is dispelled when someone suggests a dance on the turf. Many local families have gathered to welcome the team and a 'merry country-dance' ensues. The Marylebone men throw away their cigars, find partners and join the throng of couples dancing over the field while the venerable school buildings look gravely down upon them, the rooks caw in the ancient elms fringing the ground and the school flag flaps lazily in a gentle westerly breeze.

This joyous mood carries over into the cricket next day. When Marylebone's third wicket falls with only 18 runs on the board, Jack 'Swiper' Ruggles, the long-stop, cries out 'Huzza for old Rugby', stands on his head and 'brandishes his legs in the air in triumph'. A nearby fielder grabs his heels and throws him on his back. The match is closely fought but the climax of a last-over finish is intercepted by the arrival of the omnibus to take the Lord's men to the train, so the game is abandoned. Marylebone, having scored the higher total in the first innings, are declared the winners but neither side is much concerned about the result. It's the game itself that matters, as we've learnt from a boundary conversation while Rugby is batting between Tom, his close friend Arthur and 'the young Master'. Cricket, Tom remarks, is 'more than a game [...] It's an institution'. Yes, replies Arthur, it's 'the birthright of British boys old and young, as *habeas corpus* and trial by jury are of British men'.

Tom Brown's Schooldays established the public school cricket story in similar manner to Mitford's founding of the village cricket one. It captured the beginning of organised competitive sport as an important element of the reformed public school system inaugurated by Rugby's illustrious head Thomas Arnold. In the figure of 'the young Master' it offered the prototype of the schoolmaster as guide, mentor and protector of schoolboys as they grow towards manhood. Hughes's model for 'the young master' was the Reverend G.E.L. Cotton who later became Headmaster of Marlborough, a school we shall revisit later in this chapter. Cotton also served a term as Bishop of Calcutta where by introducing cricket to the missionary schools spread across his vast Indian diocese he helped make the game an essential part of the civilising mission of Empire.

The type of intimate friendship of Tom and Arthur will in later public school fiction be intensified and frequently eroticised. Hughes's novel also has echoes of war and empire, of military graves in the Crimea and India for example, where old boys of the school now lie, another theme that will become more prominent as public schoolboys go off to fight on the veldt and in the trenches.

Hughes remarks of these deaths: 'But this was not sad', which is the dominant note of subsequent treatments of this theme as the parallel between playing for your team and dying for your country is elaborated. As the young Master has said to Tom and Arthur, discipline and reliance on one another is the most valuable lesson that cricket teaches: 'It merges the individual in the eleven; he doesn't play that he may win, but that his side may'. Fighting for one's country, the public school novel will insist, is exactly the same.

Although cricket stories of the village green also shared a concern with these later wars, it is more overt in the public school story, no doubt because of the legend of the 'lost generation' of young upper-class men who fell in battle and deprived the nation of the best of its future ruling class, as well as some of its most promising cricketers. This legend was not entirely a myth. Working-class losses in the First World War, though more numerous, were proportionately lighter than those of the upper classes, and the death rate among subalterns – officers under the rank of captain who were heavily recruited from current public school pupils and recent old boys – was particularly high. The Duke of Wellington is supposed to have said that the Battle of Waterloo was won on the playing fields of Eton. Pelham Warner was scarcely more inclusive when he wrote that it was 'the public school spirit which made us come out on top in the Great War'. The deaths of so many public schoolboys sanctified this belief, and the public school cricket story which celebrated their sacrifice helped create and sustain the legend of the 'lost generation'.

H. A. Vachell's *The Hill* (1905) sealed these associations and developed the themes and tropes that *Tom Brown's Schooldays* had inaugurated, all of which are gathered together in its great set-piece chapter, 'Lord's'. The scene is the annual fixture between Harrow and Eton, dating back to the early nineteenth century, when pupils past and present come together to affirm the traditions and values of the public school ethos. As play begins, the Rev. Septimus Duff, who in his time had been three years in the Eleven, captain in his last, and whose son will this year open the bowling for his alma mater, surveys the scene: 'Upon the ground are the youth, the beauty, the rank and fashion of the kingdom, and, best of all, his old friends'.

'Forty Years On' (the name of Harrow's famous anthem), Duff and his friends have reassembled once more. The occasion is described as 'England at its best'. Coaches (four-wheeled not two-legged) circle the ground. One belongs to the Duke of Trent who, to his pride and discomfort, has sons playing in both teams; another to Charles Desmond, a cabinet minister with the threat of war in South Africa very much on his mind, and whose son, known as Caesar, is to open the batting for Harrow; a third carriage belongs to Scaife, a wealthy self-made Liverpool merchant whose 'cheques are honoured to any amount even if he isn't'. Scaife's son Reginald, 'the Demon', will be both hero and villain of the encounter, a matchless cricketer whose ill-tempered reaction to being bowled in the second innings by a ball that keeps low (he scored a century in the first) confirms he's not cut from the same cloth as his peers. 'Vitai Lampada' translates as 'They pass on the torch of life'. Scaife and his family are not part of this tradition.

The match, of course, goes down to the wire: three to make, the last man in, final ball. Eton's number 11, 'a slogger and a run-getter against village teams', is run-out by Scaife's athletic pick-up and dead-eyed throw. Harrow have won! The Rev Duff leaps to his feet, upsetting chairs and treading on toes in his excitement. But Caesar, not the Demon, is the hero of the hour. As the match had moved towards its climax, Eton's captain, whose innings seemed to be taking his team to victory, had been caught on the boundary by Caesar, a brilliant piece of fielding which the captain – that 'gallant gentleman' – had gracefully acknowledged as he made his way back to the pavilion. The contrast with Scaife's behaviour had been noted by the crowd and shared back at school. Scaife might have won the match, but Desmond had saved it, 'and the School apprehended the subtle difference'.

The first to congratulate Desmond on Harrow's victory is John Verney, the novel's protagonist. *The Hill* opens with Verney, Desmond and Scaife starting at Harrow together, and these three are the focus of Vachell's great theme, described in his dedication as the 'Romance of Friendship'. Verney is a scholar, clever, loyal and upright with a singing voice like an angel's;

Desmond is gifted at everything he touches, attractively modest but vulnerably naive; Scaife is a brilliant, hard-nosed athlete with a chip on his shoulder and a taste for danger. The rivalrous enmity between Verney and Scaife as they vie for Desmond's affection dominates the novel: Scaife is the tempter, Desmond his target, while Verney tries to protect his beloved friend from the evil Scaife embodies.

Verney's finest moment is the School Concert, another ritual occasion when the Old Boys gather. Verney is to sing the treble solo. Scaife growls that he will 'make an ass of himself', but after an uncertain start, Verney's voice soars in 'vindication of the spirit [...] unfettered by the flesh'. Desmond is rapt: 'At that moment [he] loved the singer – the singer who called to him out of heaven, who summoned his friend to join him'. Verney sings the final line of the song – three repeated notes, the last unaccompanied and 'diminishing to the merest whisper of sound' – with his gaze fixed on his friend. The School thunders applause, and one of the Old Boys, a Field Marshal no less, shouts '"Encore" as loudly as any fag'. Scaife is put out.

From this point, Desmond starts calling Verney 'Jonathan' rather than his baptismal name of John, bringing to mind the Old Testament friendship of David and Jonathan. Traditional Christian interpretation of this friendship considers it as platonic but scholars, artists and writers have seen elements of homoeroticism in the story of these two friends. Tellingly, perhaps for a novel published in 1905, Oscar Wilde at his trial in 1895 had cited the example of David and Jonathan in support of 'the love that dare not speak its name', and it had become shorthand for homosexuality among the Uranian poets, writers such as Edward Carpenter, John Addington Symonds and Lord Alfred Douglas, Wilde's nemesis. Unlike several later public school novels which took up the David and Jonathan reference, there is not a hint of physical attraction in *The Hill*. But it's difficult now, and perhaps even in 1905, to read the scene of the School Concert without feeling there is a sublimated erotic attraction in play.

Whatever kind of love it might be, its course doesn't run smooth. *The Hill* is as much about the strains of friendship as its romance. As their schooldays draw to a close, and as war in South Africa becomes inevitable, Desmond and Scaife enlist. Verney is studying for an Oxford scholarship. Desmond departs for South Africa, his face bright and eager, but for Verney, the whistle of his departing train is like a 'scream of anguish from himself'.

In the months that follow, Verney writes regularly to Desmond but gets no reply. And then a telegram from an old Harrovian at the War Office: 'Henry Desmond killed in action'. Verney is devastated. He reads and re-reads the press reports of Desmond's glorious death. Leading his men in a charge up Spion Kop 'as if he were racing for a goal', he was 'shot through the heart [...] smiling at death'. Of all those killed that day, he was the youngest by two years.

Verney's torment at being left uncertain of the truth of their friendship is finally allayed by the arrival of a letter from Desmond written on the night before his death: 'Old Jonathan, you have been the best friend a man ever had, the only one I love as much as my own brothers – *and even more*', an echo perhaps of David's letter to Jonathan in the Second Book of Samuel 1:26: 'thy love to me was wonderful, passing the love of women'. Desmond is writing looking up at the hill on which he hopes 'our flag will be waving within a few hours [...] The sight of this hill brings back our Hill [...] I shall get up the hill here faster and easier than the other fellows because you and I have so often run up our Hill together – God bless it – and you! Good night'. And thus the novel ends. The friendship of Jonathan and Desmond, so often jeopardised by Scaife, has found its apotheosis in Desmond's heroic death.

E. F. Benson's *David Blaize* (1916) makes no mention of war despite being written at its height, but is suffused with sex. Set in the later years of the nineteenth century at a time when, as Peter Burton in his introduction to the modern edition of the novel puts it, 'beautiful young men bathed naked in rivers and streams (and) played cricket under clear blue skies', its nostalgia was prompted and its popularity secured by the slaughter of young men at the time of its writing. An army major wrote to Benson from the trenches telling him of the pleasures the novel had given to his 'very fine and gallant lads', public school lads obviously.

David Blaize is another novel about the romance of friendship and cricket, with a threesome at its centre: Maddox, a gentleman, scholar, and the 'finest bat in the eleven' at the noted public school of Marchester; Hughes, David's great friend at his prep school who has gone to Marchester a year ahead of him; and David himself, a spirited but wholesome lad and promising left-arm slow bowler whose hero-worship of Maddox is 'more complete and entire than is ever accorded by the world of grown-up men and women to their most august idols'.

David's friendship with Hughes ends early in his time at Marchester when Hughes comes to sit on his bed one evening, recounts some 'filthy tale' and makes references to Maddox which leave him discomfited. David had been warned by his prep school Head as he prepared to leave for public school that he would find 'there are worse things than smoking, and all the misdeeds you may [...] have been punished for [...] even worse things than stealing [...]. Things that damn the soul, David'. But David had really no idea what the Head was talking about. Hughes has now given him an inkling.

The scene with Hughes is ended by the arrival of Maddox, who 'hoofs' him out, leaving David reassured. But a longer scene soon follows in which Maddox finds David in the bath and sits admiring him. David feels uncomfortable and Maddox ashamed, retreats to his study and sits staring at the fire. 'You damned beast', he tells himself, 'You deserve to be shot'. From now on, the sexual attraction of Maddox for his fag becomes sublimated into an intense platonic friendship based on cricket and poetry.

This temptation scene is recalled several years later when David is holidaying with Maddox and his mother somewhere on the south coast. Maddox is now 18, David 15. Lying on the sand alongside his 'pal', 'stupefied and simmering with content', we're told that David has long-suppressed the embarrassment of that earlier occasion – 'the momentary opening of a cupboard where nightmare dwelt'. The boys strip naked and plunge into the sea, swimming far out and coming to rest floating on their backs. The pleasures of the water remind Maddox of a poem he's been reading – Swinburne's 'Atalanta in Calydon' – and he quotes some lines which send David into rapture as they lie 'side by side [...] away from anything but each other and this liquid Paradise of living water'.

Back at the house, Maddox offers David the choice of Swinburne or the *Daily Telegraph* to read over lunch. David takes the paper, anxious to know how his county team, Sussex, has got on against Surrey. Maddox, however, has received news that Hughes has been expelled following the discovery of a 'disgusting and conclusive' letter he'd written to another boy in the house. Shaken, he confesses to David – 'I might have been Hughes'. Ever since that day in the bathroom, he tells David, I've 'tried instead of corrupting you, to uncorrupt myself'. By making him feel ashamed, his young friend has unwittingly been his salvation. David is left with an intense happiness such as he'd never felt before. The two then pursue a vigorous afternoon of golf, tennis and another swim before dinner, the redemptive power of sport and the safe space it offers demonstrating the purity of 'their friendship of boy-love, hot as fire and clean as the trickle of ice-water on a glacier'.

The apotheosis of their now clarified friendship is the conclusion of the House cricket final. David's house team needs 20 runs to win with two wickets remaining. Maddox is still at the crease, having batted throughout the innings. It's his last house match, and he's the last hope of his team. David has taken seven wickets, but he's no kind of batter and is anxiously hoping he won't be needed at the crease. But the ninth wicket falls, and ten runs are still needed as David walks out – his throat 'dry and gritty like the side of a match-box' – to join his friend. Maddox greets him reassuringly: 'David, old chap, isn't it ripping […] that it's you and me. Just the jolliest thing that could happen'. And so it proves. David hits an unexpected boundary, scores a lucky single and Maddox does the rest. This glorious day ends with another swim. Maddox has the sixth-form privilege of using the school pool whenever he wishes, and their housemaster gives David permission to join him: 'You blest pair of sirens', he describes them, adding to Maddox – 'take care of David, Jonathan'.

Descriptions of young men bathing together often functioned as a coded reference to homoeroticism at this time. Water was Swinburne's favourite medium and it's likely that Benson would have known of Duncan Grant's controversial mural, 'Bathing', completed in 1911 as part of a decorative scheme for the dining room at London's Borough Polytechnic. In fact, there was nothing coded about Grant's mural. Inspired by naked swimmers at the men-only Serpentine Lido in Hyde Park, it shows a group of well-muscled young men diving, swimming and clambering aboard a small boat, their poses nakedly sexualised. A writer in the *National Review* had condemned it for the corrupting influence it would have on young students. Benson, more cautious than Grant, exploits the association of naked bathing with homosexual culture at this time while simultaneously cleansing it of such associations. In his 1915 poem, 'Peace', Rupert Brooke had thanked God for matching the young men of England with a war that would rouse them from sleeping, describing the opportunity as being like 'swimmers into cleanness leaping'. Swimming for Maddox and David is similarly purifying.

In Benson's novel, cricket, like bathing, provides a sublimated arena in which homoerotic feelings can be expressed and its temptations suppressed. On Maddox's last day at Marchester, he and David meet below the pavilion and stand looking across the ground. The idyll of their friendship is about to end. Maddox reminds David that at least they're not dead, the only moment in the novel when even a veiled, if anachronistic, reference is made to the First World War. David tells Maddox that he'll never have another friend like him. Maddox says that he'd better not, to which David responds: 'I suppose we're rather idiots about each other'. Maddox immediately turns the conversation towards cricket: 'Look at the pitch there! What a lot of ripping hours it's given to generations of fellows, me among them.' A hallowed and redemptive place.

When Maddox departs for Cambridge, the novel takes a sudden heterosexual turn. David is briefly smitten with someone his friend Bags calls 'a female girl', but when asked by his friend whether he'd rather kiss Violet Gray or see the Oxford and Cambridge match, he pauses. The question repeats the moment when Maddox had asked him to choose between Swinburne and the *Daily Telegraph* cricket report. Once again he opts for cricket, especially if Maddox is going to score a century.

The novel ends with David, grievously injured after trying to stop a runaway horse and cart, being visited by Maddox, who sits all night at his bedside holding his hand and restoring him to life. Such is the depth and power of male friendship.

Alec Waugh's *The Loom of Youth* (1917) is something of a curiosity in the tradition of public school fiction. Waugh, older brother of the more famous novelist Evelyn, was expelled from Sherborne School in 1915 for having too intimate a friendship with another boy. Still only 17, he wrote *The Loom of Youth* over three months while in an army training camp, and it was published just as he was posted to France as a second lieutenant, a subaltern. It was well received by reviewers such as J. C. Squire, the model for William Hodge, captain of The Invalids in *England, Their England* (Waugh himself was the original of the novelist Robert Southcott in Macdonell's cricket match – 'a singular young man in perfectly creamed white flannels, white silk socks, a pale pink silk shirt and a white cap') and by C. K. Scott-Moncrieff, Proust's first translator, but angrily denounced by public school heads and teachers. A former Head of Eton described it as 'pernicious stuff', and Waugh received pained letters of rebuke from the Head of Sherborne and the school's sports master, both of whom figure prominently and unmistakably in the novel as themselves.

In his preface to a later edition of the novel, Waugh wrote: 'No book before [...] had accepted as part of the fabric of School life the inevitable consequences of a monastic herding together for eight months of the year of thirteen year old children and eighteen year old adolescents.' In fact same-sex relations were not the main cause of outrage. Waugh's treatment of the subject is less prominent than in *David Blaize*. It was the novel's criticisms of the public school system's harmful 'blind worship of games' that provoked the indignation and ensured its success. It went through four reprints in six months and was regularly reprinted in the years that followed.

For all this, *The Loom of Youth* is full of long detailed accounts of cricket and football (that is, rugby) matches, close finishes and the triumphs of victory. The transparently autobiographical protagonist, Gordon Caruthers, is a leader in both sports, and although he comes to understand the hollowness of the public school culture of games, his criticisms are softened and qualified by an enduring affection for it. This is plangently expressed in the novel's final scene, another of the close-of-play tableaux that are a feature of this genre as a whole: '"It will be a long time before we have as wonderful a time again", Gordon said, as he passed in the sunset, for the last time, through the gate of the cricket-field which had been, for him, the place of so many happy hours'. Cricket remains untouched by Waugh's discontent with a system that expelled him and withheld his First XI batting cup, awarded for a season's average of 32.5. The redeeming quality of cricket somehow persists.

The narrator of *David Blaize* remarks on the self-contained world of the public school: 'Everything that might happen after public school was over seemed a post-humous sort of affair.' Ernest Raymond's novel *Tell England: A Study in a Generation* (1922) shows that for the First World War generation of public schoolboys, this was literally so. Its narrator, Rupert Ray, has completed the manuscript of his novel in a dug-out on the night before he is killed going over the top to attack the German lines. The manuscript has been recovered and edited by a padre who had been with Ray at Gallipoli three years earlier.

Tell England is the classic public school novel of this period, bringing together all the themes associated with cricket found in its predecessors: friendship, sex, war, nation and death. Like many of its predecessors, it also presents a problem of how to read a novel that is both coy and explicit, innocent and knowing, repressed and passionate.

In an early scene of *Tell England*, the 13-year-old protagonist Ray and his best chum Doe are caned by the assistant housemaster Radley, the finest bat in the Middlesex team, 'a man of over six feet, with the shoulder, chest, and waist of a forcing batsman'. At Ray's fourth stroke, 'an especially resounding one', one of the class murmurs: 'Well, *that's* a boundary anyway.' In the dormitory that evening, Doe, who has often been teased as Radley's favourite, confesses to Ray there is no one in the world he likes more than Radley and that he'd 'simply loved being whacked by him'. Having confessed this, Doe turns red and the conversation goes no further, but Ray, lying back on his pillow, fantasises about his friend as a girl, 'with his hair, paler than straw, reaching down beneath his shoulders, and with his brown eyes and parted lips wearing a feminine appearance'. He begins to feel, 'somewhere in the region of my waist', a 'calf-love' for the girl he's imagined. But then he recalls Doe's prowess at cricket, 'his gender became conclusively established, and – ah well, I was half asleep'. Cricket has once again saved the day.

Not conclusively, however. Soon after, Ray is watching Doe at the crease, and a particularly stylish cover drive leaves him with a 'squirmy sensation at the thought that he was my especial friend [...] the wind was playing with his hair, his shirt sleeves were rolled up, showing arms smooth and round like a woman's'. Ray will later remember this scene, Doe standing out amidst 'the flannelled figures of the players, with their wide little chests, neat waists, and round hips, [who] promised fine things for the manhood of England ten years on'.

Tell England, like all public school novels, features a Great Match in which the hero wins the day. In this case, it is the annual School versus Masters fixture which, because of Radley, the Masters have won for the last eight years. This year, however, the School team is led by a rising star, the Hon. F. Lancaster, 'who appeared for a few moments like a new comet in the cricket heavens, just as the thundercloud of war blotted everything out. When the cloud should roll away, that new comet would be no longer there'. The Eleven has had a remarkable year, even defeating a strong visiting MCC team, and the School's hopes are high. Ray, with his loopy leg-breaks, is a surprise last-minute inclusion in the team. Come the last innings, the Masters need either to bat out time or score 250 in two-and-a-half hours. Radley takes charge until, with ten minutes left, only 14 runs are required. The school starts shouting for Ray to be given a bowl, and a cry is taken up: 'Hoo-*Ray*, hoo-*Ray*, hoo-blooming-*Ray*'! Lancaster defers to the cry. Radley is facing. Ray's first ball is a wide; his second and third go for boundaries. The School groans. But Radley fumbles and misses the fourth, and as Ray runs in to deliver the next, he is suddenly confident that 'the supreme moment of my schooldays was upon me'. Radley is beaten, and his leg bail falls to the ground. The chant of 'hoo-*Ray*' continues for the next half-hour.

The following chapter begins: 'It was on the day those two pistol shots were fired at an Austrian Archduke in the streets of Sarajevo that the Masters' match was played out at Kensingtowe'. The shadow of impending war hangs over Part One of the novel – 'Five Gay Years of School' – and becomes the reality of Part Two – 'Now the Rest – War'. Lancaster is not the only young man that day whose fate is anticipated and mourned. Moles White, scorer of an ungainly and unlikely half-century, is cheered back to the pavilion, 'a final picture, which our memory preserves of White alive [...] Grand old boy, may we meet many more like you'. Several years later, at Gallipoli, Ray and Doe will come across his grave – Lieutenant R. White, Royal Dublin Fusiliers – with an epitaph which gives the novel its name: 'Tell England, ye who pass this monument, WE died for her, and here we rest content'.

But this is still to come. A couple of days after the Great Match, Ray calls on Radley to say goodbye. It is the end of term. Radley is in a sombre mood, cast down by the approaching war of which Ray is almost oblivious. Told by Radley that within a few days England will be at war with Germany, he responds: 'Oh, what fun! We'll give 'em no end of a thrashing. I hate Germans.' As he leaves the room, Radley stands at the window 'staring out [...] over the empty cricket fields', a scene frequently repeated in cricket fiction, elegiac and nostalgic, capturing the sweet sorrow of the close of play.

The treatment of war in Book II of *Tell England* follows a similar outline to that of the war poets of the period, from excited anticipation to belated realisation of its horrors. Rupert Ray's eagerness, and Rupert Brooke's celebration of its onset as an opportunity for the young men of England to fulfil their glorious destiny, is echoed by the colonel who welcomes Ray and Doe into his regiment as commissioned officers:

Your birth and breeding were given you that you might officer England's youth in this hour. And now you enter upon your inheritance. Just as this is *the* day in the history of the world so yours is *the* generation. No other generation has been called to such grand things, and to such crowded glorious living.

When the two hear of the death of a former school-fellow and Doe laments the unfairness of it, the colonel takes down a book of poems from his shelf and reads from it:

'These laid the world away; poured out the red
Sweet wine of youth; gave up the years to be
Of hope and joy [...]
Blow, bugles, blow [...]
Nobleness walks in our ways again'

The poem is unnamed and the lines slightly misquoted, but they are from Brooke's sonnet 'The Dead', which ends, 'And we have come into our heritage'. The torch of life and young death has been passed on.

The sexual theme carries over from Part One. The colonel, like other mentors in these novels, tells Ray and Doe to 'take pride in your bodies, and hold them in condition [...] There are more ways than one of getting them tainted in the life of temptations you're going to face'. One evening, on board ship approaching Gallipoli, celebrations break out at the news that British forces have taken Suvla Bay. There is drinking, singing and dancing. One of the subalterns seizes Doe around the waist and, 'clasping the slim youth to him, leads the boy (who's as graceful as a girl and as sinuous as a serpent) through the voluptuous movements of the latest dance [...] seductive, tantalising, enticing'. The scene recalls Ray watching Doe batting at prep school.

Weeks later at Gallipoli, they prepare for an attack on the Turkish defences. Doe is to lead his men in the charge while Ray's soldiers provide covering fire. Ray knows that Doe, with 'his passion for the heroic', would never hold back 'like a diffident batsman in his block. He would reach the opposite crease, or be run out'. And so it proves. Our last picture of Doe is at the top of the hill they're attempting to take. As Ray watches through the smoke, Doe stops and staggers back – he's been shot: 'His cap fell off, and the wind blew his hair about, as it used to do on the cricket-field at school. He recovered an upright position; he smiled very clearly – then folded up, and collapsed.' Gallipoli is like a cricket match gloriously lost.

But by now, the mood of the novel is closer to Wilfred Owen than to Brooke. Owen's poem 'Greater Love' takes its title from John 15:13: 'Greater love hath no man than this, that a man lay down his life for his friend.' The poem figures romantic love as a woman whose seductive power is as nothing compared to the love of comrades and the passionate sacrifice of the soldier killed in battle. From its opening lines – 'Red lips are not so red / As the stained stones kissed by the English dead' – this love is sexualised. Brooke's 'red sweet wine of youth' has been transfigured into the red blood of doomed youth, but the protracted sibilance of the second line makes sacrifice itself seductive and alluring. It is the bonds of love between men as much as love of one's nation that the poem celebrates.

The passion of Ray's loss and mourning of Doe echoes this: 'In the freshness of my loss, I thought no lover had ever loved as I did. "I loved you – I loved you – I loved you," I repeated. And I even worked myself up into a weary longing to die'. It is then that the padre who will later edit Ray's manuscript insists: 'Tell England – You must write a book and tell 'em, Rupert, about the dead schoolboys of your generation'. The text then repeats the inscription on Lieutenant White's grave: 'Tell England, ye who pass this monument, We died for her, and here we rest content'.

The message of Ray's manuscript, however, is more complex than that of Moles White's epitaph, which brings me back around to the question of how to read a novel such as this: How self-aware is it? How coded? How innocent? And what is the novel trying to tell England?

A helpful point of reference is T. C. Worsley's memoir *Flannelled Fool* (1967), his account of schooldays at Marlborough College in the 1920s (where 'the young Master' in *Tom Brown's Schooldays* became Head, where E. F. Benson was educated, and the model of the school in *David Blaize*), and of his subsequent years as a schoolmaster at Wellington College. Worsley writes of his adoring friendship at Marlborough with an older boy, the captain of cricket:

> I didn't think of him, let me say, in any sexual connection. I didn't at that time even know I could. But I was content only in his company – I might almost say, alive only when with him. And since cricket was the centre of his life, as of mine – in the holidays as well as in the term – that summer when he took possession of my feelings, had been idyllic.

The telling sentence here is Worsley's ignorance of such a thing as same-sex attraction, which also informs other passionate friendships of youth in these novels. Worsley's innocence is genuine and, as he describes it, persisted for a remarkably long time. Cricket helped in this. Worsley was a talented wicketkeeper and batter who played for Cambridge University and whose sporting prowess had secured him his post at Wellington after he'd graduated with a poor degree. The 'close-knit fellowship' he enjoyed as a member of the eleven at Marlborough had, he wrote, 'a kind of homo-erotic liaison binding it together', although he concedes that no one else would have felt this as strongly as he did. But, he continues, 'behind the pretence of virility which cricket and other games supplied […] was my repression of sexual potency […] It enabled me to escape noticing what in fact was missing. The generalised homo-eroticism which I discovered in the rituals of the playing fields satisfied my inclinations enough to keep them "pure"'.

For Worsley, sport in general and cricket in particular was a prophylactic against homosexuality. Repression and sublimation are intimate bedfellows. But as the scene where Ray watches Doe batting shows, cricket could also be a means of experiencing and expressing same-sex attraction in a remarkably open manner.

Simon Raven's novel *Fielding Gray* (1967), and his memoir *Shadows on the Grass* (1982), which makes clear the autobiographical basis of the novel and which E. W. Swanton described as 'the filthiest book on cricket' he'd ever read, is entirely without the hesitations, ambivalence, displacements or repression of previous fiction of this genre. In breaking open the codes which lie half-hidden in its predecessors, it marks the end of the road for the public school cricket story.

One of these is 'the pash', which Raven describes 'as an abiding if scarcely a wholesome element in school life […] which any boy might entertain for another, usually a younger one'. Fielding Gray has no truck with the 'petty guilt and assorted silliness' that surrounds this. His desire for Christopher Roland is too strong to be 'demeaned by the idiom of the lower fourth', and so it proves when Fielding takes Roland to the dark tower of a hayloft.

The shadow of Oscar Wilde's novel *The Picture of Dorian Gray* (1891) hangs over public school cricket fiction. Doe's full name is Edgar Gray Doe, and his school nickname is the Gray Doe. When Ray joins Doe at his family home in Falmouth where Radley is also a guest, his friend and the teacher meet him at the station. Doe is 'hanging on his [teacher's] arm' and wearing a light grey suit, an exact copy of one that Radley had worn during the previous term. Wilde's novel is also referred to in *David Blaize*, and I take it that Benson is teasing those of his readers in the know when he names the young woman, that 'female girl' David is briefly infatuated with before he and Maddox are reunited, Violet Gray. The surname of Raven's eponymous hero makes explicit the 'decadence' that previous fiction had only hinted at and, through his forename, mischievously associates it with cricket. Fielding had been named after an old friend of his mother's killed in the First World War, a keen cricketer nicknamed Fielding because his surname was Legge. Only swimming is missing from the serious fun the novel has with the conventions of the public school genre. From all accounts, Raven, a dedicated drinker described by the founder of the *Paris Review*, George Plimpton, as 'an unmade bed of a man', had an aversion to water in all its uses.

Fielding Gray opens with a scene that rewrites the genre's explicit patriotism. It is the second Sunday after the Second World War has ended and there's a service in the Charterhouse school chapel to remember the fallen. Old boys of the school have turned out in numbers but not this time for a cricket match. Fielding, a sixth-former at the school, provides a sardonic commentary on the proceedings which begin with 'a spirited rendering of "Jerusalem", the political implications of which escaped most present set[ting] up a smug sense of triumph'. Then follows a roll-call of the dead. As the list goes on and on, Fielding wonders if it will ever stop: 'All right, so they're all dead. What good will it do them or anybody else to carry on about it?'

The headmaster angers his audience by telling them that 'the old way of life' is over but the war isn't: 'The enormity has been too great; the residue of guilt is so vast that we must all bear our share of it. We cannot retire into our pleasant gardens to sit at leisure while the world's wound festers outside our wall'. This provokes 'resentful muttering among the officers' but the mood is lifted by the organist breaking into 'The day Thou gavest, Lord, has ended'. The officers relax into the familiar hymn while the boys 'bellow happily away in a sentimental trance [...] It was a communion on the lowest possible level, a common agreement to wipe out an intolerable debt with the liquid of a few easy tears'. The scene ends with the words – 'Tell England with the drum and with the bugle: these, your sons, are dead' – a bitter echo of Ernest Raymond's novel.

We first glimpse Christopher Roland that same afternoon in the chapel as Fielding seeks distraction from the catalogue of the dead: 'wavy tow hair; square creamy forehead; mild eyes, wide-set, and soft nose; full lips curved slightly downwards; dented chin'. Fielding had first noticed him a few months earlier leaving the Fives Courts: 'cheeks flushed, stockings down over ankles […] shorts (because of clothes rationing) noticeably outgrown'. Christopher had smiled and waved, leaving Fielding staring after him at 'someone graceful and kind and gay […] who had waved me a share of his grace, smiled me a portion of his gaiety, as he passed in the evening light'.

On the evening of the memorial service, 'a seemly sing-song' arranged to honour the day morphs into something very different. One moment, the boys of the House are singing 'The Lincolnshire Poacher', the next a gramophone is playing 'Jealousy' and the 'elder half of the House was coupled with the younger in a shambling, sweaty tango', an obvious reference to the troopship scene in *Tell England*. Fielding dances with Christopher, and on the way back to their respective dormitories they take each other's hand.

Fielding's attraction to Christopher is soon transferred to the cricket field. His century against Eton is 'all the sweeter' for having Christopher, who scores 47, at the other end. When the Scholars play the Rest of the School – the great match of this novel – they are on opposite sides. Fielding is less concerned that his team, the Scholars, should win than that Christopher should do well. He delights in watching Christopher batting: 'Hair bleached by the sun […] arms brown and smooth, fair, delicate skin showing through the cleft of his unbuttoned shirt'. He admires Christopher's graceful footwork and timing and describes the moment when bat meets ball in distinctively sexual terms: 'that thrilling moment of impact when the hard leather sinks, briefly but luxuriously, into the sprung willow, and the swift current of joy quivers up the blade and on through every nerve in the body'.

Raven himself was a more than useful cricketer. At prep school, he had clean bowled a future England captain, David Sheppard; he played with another future captain of England, Peter May, in the Charterhouse 1st Eleven; and scored 41 for the school in its match against the MCC. However, the Scholars versus School match in *Fielding Gray* is of secondary importance. It's the aftermath of the match that matters. Fielding takes Christopher down a path through some woods to a hayloft. It's July and the hay is 'still sweet', not yet 'dry and prickly'. They undress and lie down together. The sex leaves both of them unhappy – Christopher accusatory, Fielding guilty and unsatisfied – but it's the explicit nature of the encounter that most striking. In previous novels, swimming has been the coded way of describing same-sex physical passion: in *David Blaize* where, as here, it follows success on the cricket field, and in *Tell England* where Ray and Doe, on holiday in Falmouth, enjoy naked swimming and diving contests in a scene that recalls Maddox and David at the coast. In *Fielding Gray* we get total immersion.

Raven rewrites other dominant conventions of the genre. Fielding's only interest in the outcome is seducing Christopher. Team spirit is entirely absent, and the conventions of sportsmanship are no longer adhered to. Christopher is given out one short of a century for handing the ball back to the bowler, a malicious decision from Fielding's antagonist, Somerset Lloyd-Jones, who is umpiring, and the Scholars win. Somerset Lloyd-Jones is transparently based on another contemporary of Raven's at Charterhouse, his main rival as a Classics scholar, William Rees-Mogg, future editor of *The Times*, vice-chair of the BBC, and father of Jacob.

Most of all, the novel rewrites the sacred bonds of friendship, which is the overriding theme of Vachell, Benson and Raymond's novels. Raven's great theme, here and in much of his other work, is betrayal. In *Fielding Gray* this results in Lloyd-James's Machiavellian plotting, Christopher's suicide and Fielding's rejection by his solid and trustworthy friend, Peter Morrisson, for having failed all his friends in love. The romance of friendship is dead. Its strains which give those earlier novels their tension are now irredeemable. The passionate bonding of youth will not mature into lifelong friendship. Forty years on, indeed much sooner, all that has vanished.

Eric Midwinter, in *Quill on Willow*, described cricket in public school stories as a form of brainwashing to inculcate the values of manliness. He must be thinking here of the popular periodical tradition dating from the launch of *The Boy's Own Paper* (BOP) in 1879, and its successors such as *Chums*, *The Gem* and *The Magnet*, with its offshoots in book form, of which Talbot Baines Reed's *The Fifth Form at St. Dominics* is the most famous example.

The tradition I've been discussing, while not entirely distinct from that of the boys' periodical, is more literary, by which I mean it is less hackneyed, stereotyped and pulpy, and treats cricket in more complex and interesting ways. George Orwell, in his essay 'Boys' Weeklies' described the mental world of the BOP tradition:

The year is 1910 – or 1940, but it is all the same. You are [...] sitting down to tea in your study [...] after an exciting game of football which was won by an odd goal in the last half-minute. There is a cosy fire in the study and outside the wind is whistling. The ivy clusters thickly around the old grey stones. The King is on his throne and the pound is worth a pound. Over in Europe the comic foreigners are jabbering and gesticulating [...] Everything is safe, solid and unquestionable. Everything will be the same for ever and ever.

The keynote of this passage is that time stands still. The keynote of the novels I've been considering is that nothing is altogether safe, solid and unquestionable. War and its aftermath has wrought deep disturbances, nation can no longer be taken for granted and 'chums' is an incomplete description of male friendship.

Chapter 3

THE CRICKET MURDER STORY

There was no denying the fact that people had been killed at cricket.

–Hugh De Sélincourt

No man who could bat like that would commit a mean and cowardly murder.

–Nicholas Blake

E. W. Hornung was the first writer of fiction to explicitly connect cricket with crime. His collection of stories, *The Amateur Cracksman* (1899), featured the public school gentleman, cricketer and criminal, A. J. Raffles, a character suggested to him by his brother-in-law Arthur Conan Doyle. After reading Hornung's Australian novel *Irralie's Bushranger* (1895), about a monocled bushranger, Doyle remarked that 'a public-school villain would be a new figure for a series'. He wasn't altogether happy with the result, however, writing to Hornung that although 'there are few finer examples of short-story writing [...] I think they are rather dangerous in their suggestion [...] You must not make a criminal a hero'. What a pity that Doyle never included cricket in one of his Sherlock Holmes stories.

In any of the public school cricket stories I've discussed, Raffles would have been the school cad, a bounder, not a hero. He is a jewel thief who uses his public school education and particularly his cricketing prowess as the cover he needs to forage among the gemstones of Mayfair society. As he remarks to his companion in crime, his former fag at Uppingham, Bunny: 'I'd chuck up cricket tomorrow [...] if it wasn't for the glorious protection it affords a person of my proclivities', adding 'it's the one and only reason why I don't burn my bats for firewood'.

Raffles' attitude to cricket is at the heart of his paradoxical character. Playing for the Gentlemen at Lord's in the third of *The Amateur Cracksman* stories, 'Gentlemen and Players', he is described as 'a dangerous bat, a brilliant field, and perhaps the very finest slow bowler of his decade'. But he only ever attends Lord's when he is playing and has no particular interest in cricket when he's not. As he explains to Bunny: 'What's the satisfaction of taking a man's wicket when you want his spoons. Still, if you can bowl a bit your low cunning won't get rusty, and always looking for the weak spot's just the kind of mental exercise one wants'.

But there's also no keener cricketer on the field, no one more anxious to perform well for his team. In the nets at the start of the season, he places sovereigns on the stumps, remarking that professionals will bowl like demons for hard cash. His bowling style reflects the complexity of his character: 'His perfect command of pitch and break, his beautifully easy action, which never varied with the varying pace, his great ball on the leg stump – his dropping head ball'. This latter is a ball commonly described in cricket fiction of the early twentieth century, in Ian Hay's *Pip* (1907) for example, and memorably in Conan Doyle's 'The Story of Spedegue's Dropper' (1928) in which a village cricketer is plucked from obscurity to win an Ashes test bowling lobs. It is a style still often seen in village cricket. Bunny, watching Raffles at Lord's and enjoying the 'intellectual treat' and 'athletic prowess' of his friend's bowling, understands the affinity between cricket and crime: 'the combination of resource and cunning, of patience and precision, of head-work and handiwork, which made every over an artistic whole'.

'Gentlemen and Players' is Hornung's most intricate weaving together of cricket and crime. During the Lord's match he has been invited by Lord Amersteth to join the cricket week he's arranging at his country estate, Milchester Abbey in Dorset, to celebrate his son's coming of age. There will be a series of matches against the Free Foresters, the Dorsetshire Gentlemen and 'some local lot as well'. Raffles quickly realises that this 'swagger house-party' will offer 'a houseful of diamonds' and although he claims to be strict about never abusing his position as a guest, he resents being treated as a cricketer for hire, like a hired waiter or the member of a band, and overcomes his rather flexible scruples.

Raffles typically keeps his companion in the dark about his plans, but at the grand dinner that opens the cricket week, Bunny notices the necklace of diamonds and sapphires about the ample neck of the Dowager Marchioness of Melrose and realises why Raffles has tolerated the indignity of being treated like a professional. Also in the mix is an undercover detective posing as a guest and, in the neighbourhood nearby, one of the cleverest thieves in London. Raffles's combined skills as criminal and cricketer enable him to take advantage of the situation. 'Set A to watch B, and he won't have an eye left for C', as he explains to Bunny, comparing it to a Gentleman and Players single-wicket match (a popular form of the game at this time). With Raffles as the gentleman and the other criminal the professional, the field is set to mislead the detective.

On the final night of the cricket week, the jewel-case is taken, the inspector shot and Raffles by a sleight of hand secures the necklace. Crawshay, the professional thief, has been outwitted at his own game by the amateur thief, Raffles. The penultimate story of *The Amateur Cracksman*, in which Crawshay returns to take his revenge, is titled 'The Return Match'.

Throughout these stories, Hornung emphasises the similarities between cricket and crime through his recurring use of cricketing figures of speech. When Raffles and Bunny resume their partnership in crime in the rather inferior sequel collection, the *Further Adventures of the Amateur Cracksman* (1901), Bunny describes this as 'our second innings'. It is 20 years later, they score a few 'singles' but their 'best shots […] [now] go straight to hand', and they find they're 'playing a deuced slow game'. This leads to the final Raffles story, 'The Knee of the Gods', where he and Bunny depart England for South Africa to fight in the 'Boer War'. In a similar manner to public school stories of going to war, cricket provides the language to describe death in battle. The tossing of grenades is likened to bowling and, as Bunny lies wounded, Raffles comes to the aid of his comrade in theft and war by firing at a Boer soldier in 'a grey felt hat at deep long-on'. But the hat is a blind, as Raffles realises just before he himself is killed: 'The crafty cuss, he must have stuck it up on purpose. Another over […] scoring's slow […] His hat-trick's foolish'. Raffles's final words are a run of demented cricketing metaphors.

George Orwell, in his essay 'Raffles and Miss Blandish' (1944), contrasts the difference in moral atmosphere between Hornung's gentlemanly turn-of-the-century crime stories and the American crime writer James Hadley Chase's brutal *Miss Blandish*, published in 1939. The comparison is deftly made but rather obvious. More interesting is Orwell's scrutiny of the morally equivocal codes of cricket and gentlemanly conduct that characterise the Raffles stories. Cricket, he writes, 'is a game of forlorn hopes and sudden dramatic changes of fortune, and its rules are so ill-defined that their interpretation is partly an ethical business'. He gives the example of bodyline where Larwood 'was not actually breaking any rule: he was merely doing something that was "not cricket"'.

The sporting concept of 'playing the game' and the gentlemanly idea of 'good form' are the ambiguous core of the Raffles stories, values that Hornung puts under pressure in the character of his hero, who made Conan Doyle so uneasy. As a cricketer, Raffles would always play the game, but the game itself is his cover for crime. On the one hand, Raffles's chivalrous attitude to the game is the mark of a true amateur; a gentleman should not take winning too seriously. But, on the other, Raffles's relaxed attitude to sport extends to areas of life where it shouldn't.

The theft of the Dowager Marchioness's necklace technically accords with Raffles's code never to steal from his host, but it is also an abuse of hospitality based on resentment at Lord Amersteth for treating him like a hired hand. Another part of his code is that he never kills anyone, but this is not strictly true either. Raffles does kill a man and is largely responsible for the death of two others; it just happens that they're foreigners who've behaved reprehensively. And as for his claim to be patriotic, although in the story 'A Jubilee Present' he sends the Queen – 'the finest sovereign the world has ever seen' – an antique cup, it just happens to be a treasure he's stolen from the British Museum.

Another example of Raffles's patriotism, Orwell argues, is that when the Boer War begins to go badly, 'his one thought is to find his way into the fighting line' where he dies gloriously by a Boer bullet. But this isn't really why Raffles and Bunny join the South African Field Force. Raffles's cover has been blown and his field of crime shut down. The shoot-out which leaves Raffles dead and Bunny 'more or less lame for life' is more like the last hurrah of Butch Cassidy and the Sundance Kid than the glorious deaths decorated with heroic sporting metaphors we have seen in *The Hill* and *Tell England*. Diamonds might be a man's best friend but they've turned out not to be forever. The treatment of Raffles's death is more personal than patriotic, and unlike Watson's war wound which is psychologically healed by meeting Holmes, Bunny's wound signifies an empty future without his patron.

As Hornung's contemporaries would have recognised, one of the models for the character of Raffles was George Cecil Ives, a writer, sex psychologist, criminologist, penal reformer and gifted amateur cricketer who played regularly alongside Hornung in J. M. Barrie's motley team of writer-cricketers, the Allahakbarries. He played one first-class game, for the MCC at Lord's alongside Conan Doyle. Ives loved swimming. Like Raffles, he had rooms in the Albany, as did Oscar Wilde, a personal friend. Ernest Worthington, the almost eponymous hero of Wilde's play *The Importance of Being Earnest*, also lives in the Albany. Ives was discreetly homosexual, had a brief affair with Lord Alfred Douglas and founded a secret society called the 'Order of Chaeronea' for those of similar sexual orientation. Hornung was heterosexual but sympathetic to the world of the Albany, as evidenced by naming his son, born just one week before the start of Wilde's ill-judged libel case against the Marquess of Queensberry, Oscar. The Albany continued to provide a coded reference to homosexuality in twentieth-century fiction. In *Mrs Dalloway*, for example, there is 'Little Mr Bowley, who had rooms in the Albany and was sealed with wax over the deeper sources of life', and we shall see a similar use of the Albany later in this chapter.

There is nothing explicitly homosexual about the relationship of Raffles and Bunny, but it is certainly closer, more intimate and emotionally complex than that of their lightly parodied prototypes Holmes and Watson. C. P. Snow, writing in 1957, puts it well: 'It is not erotic, but it has homosexual undertones about which Hornung was not in the slightest inhibited. He just reveals that here was a kind of love.'

Raffles is an aesthete as well as an athlete, a cricketing dandy, a not uncommon figure at this time. Kevin Telfer has described how cricket followed the upper and middle-class fashions of the *fin-de-siecle*: 'The men wore smartly pressed flannels and many amateurs emulated Ranjitsinhji by donning a silk shirt. Brightly coloured silk ties were worn around the waist instead of belts and there were garishly striped caps and blazers of a variety of different colours'. The Zingari blazer Raffles is wearing in 'Gentleman and Players' (I Zingari or I.Z. was the oldest of the wandering cricket clubs of this time, bizarrely taking its name from the Italian word for gypsies) is of black, red and gold stripes, as was the club cap. There was nothing outré about such dress. Even the emphatically Victorian W. G. Grace wore a brightly coloured scarf around his bulging waist.

Nevertheless, as always with Hornung's supple and playful imagination, there is something paradoxical, even Wildean, about Raffles. The moral equivocation of the stories Orwell draws attention to is never seriously resolved in the way he suggests. Raffles remains a contradictory character, not so much the alternation of Jekyll with Hyde as a queer mixture of the two. In the final chapter of Stevenson's novel, 'Henry Jekyll's Full Statement of the Case', Jekyll hazards a guess that rather than man being simply two, he 'will be ultimately known for a mere polity of multifarious, incongruous and independent denizens'. In creating Raffles, it's as if Hornung has imbibed something of this suggestion, good and bad being so inseparably mixed that the terms themselves come into question. And cricket, a game Hornung deeply loved, is part of this strange compound.

Crime stories before the First World War didn't always involve murder. The earliest crime mystery by an English novelist, Wilkie Collins' *The Moonstone* (1868) (the American writer Edgar Allan Poe has the best claim to have invented the detective story) involved the theft of a valuable Indian diamond of great religious significance. Jewel theft also features in other writings of the period, such as Anthony Trollope's *The Eustace Diamonds* (1871). After the war, however, crime stories almost invariably involved murder, a trend that came to influence cricket fiction too. This period – the golden age of the English murder mystery – was ushered in by a famous quartet of women novelists – Agatha Christie, Dorothy L. Sayers, Margery Allingham and Ngaio Marsh – and in like manner the cricket murder mystery also included many women writers.

Apart from murder, the other striking difference between the Raffles stories and crime writing after the First World War is that the latter focuses on the detective rather than the criminal. Even Christie's most famous mystery *The Murder of Roger Ackroyd* (1926), in which the narrator proves to be the murderer, is a Poirot novel. Hornung, nevertheless, was a point of reference for later exponents of the cricket murder mystery. Raffles is an obvious prototype of Sayers' upper-class cricket-playing amateur detective Lord Peter Wimsey, just as Wimsey in turn was the initially parodied model for Allingham's gentleman-sleuth Albert Campion. Christie used Hornung's invented name of Milchester for the village and abbey in 'Gentleman and Players' in two of her novels, and in Barbara Worsley-Gough's novel *Alibi Innings* (1954) the prime suspect is a young man obsessed with jewels who lives in the Albany.

For all that cricket plays such a significant role in the Raffles's stories, it is never directly part of a crime. Hornung's successors, however, saw the possibilities offered by a cricket match for committing a murder, although it's around the boundary rather than out in the middle where the crime is committed. I've tried without success to think of a convincing way to secretly and deliberately murder someone while actually playing the game. But the setting, where the spectators' attention is fixed on the game, or on a long hot afternoon has drifted off into sleep, is full of possibilities. A cricket ground is larger and more informal than a country house, but it is nevertheless an enclosed and tranquil space, and a crowd offers a long list of suspects. A game of cricket can also provide excellent cover for a detective investigating a murder.

Cricket takes a lot of time, and the slowly unfolding nature of a match also suits the form of the novel. Both share similarities of pace and rhythm, short moments of dramatic action punctuated by long periods of slow build-up in which nothing much seems to happen, and the accumulating tension which quickens as a solution or a result is neared. And not only place and time but also character, the third fundamental component of the novel. Whether at Lord's or on the village green, cricket offers a cast of different types and styles, shapes and ages, more possibilities for idiosyncrasy and a range of suspects than other sports, to animate the narrative and its denouement.

Dorothy L. Sayers knew her cricket. Her upper-class amateur sleuth, Lord Peter Death Bredon Wimsey, DSO, Eton and Oxford, who features in 11 of her novels, played cricket for his university, where he also took a first in history. Wimsey is an expert on food and wine, early books, classical music and an accomplished pianist. He drives a 12-cylinder 1927 Daimler, black of course. Cricket figures in passing in several of the novels and centrally in *Murder Must Advertise* (1933), where an inter-office cricket match in which Wimsey is playing holds the clue that will establish the identity of the murderer.

Wimsey is easily ridiculed or deplored. Edmund Wilson, the American writer and critic, dismissed him as 'a dreadful [...] English nobleman of the casual and debonair kind, with [an] embarrassing name', while George Orwell, a little more subtly, suggested that the gentle irony with which Sayers treats her hero and his noble ancestors enables her 'to lay on the snobbishness ('his lordship' etc.) more thickly than any overt snob would dare to'. Sayers herself described Wimsey as a mixture of Fred Astaire and Bertie Wooster, which better describes the light touch with which he is treated. Neither Wilson nor Orwell saw the generic similarities between Wimsey and Raffles, aspects of which were later developed by Ian Fleming in the Bond novels, and both ignored Wimsey's backstory. Blown up and buried in a shell-hole in France in 1918, he'd returned to England suffering from a serious and prolonged breakdown, post-traumatic stress disorder as we would call it. Wimsey is not the ninny that the two critics made out, at least not unconsciously so – he's a man of masks. Nor does Sayers herself fit the type often ascribed to her, as her picture in the National Portrait Gallery, smoking and wearing a jacket and tie, makes clear.

Sayers confessed in a letter to her publisher Victor Gollancz that she didn't think much of *Murder Must Advertise*: 'The new book is nearly done. I hate it because it isn't the one I wanted to write, but I had to shove it in because I couldn't get the technical dope on *The Nine Tailors* in time'. *The Nine Tailors*, a murder mystery set in the Cambridgeshire Fens about a group of church bell-ringers, is perhaps her best novel, but *Murder Must Advertise* is more interesting than her dismissive account suggests, not least in the way cricket is used to solve a mystery and incorporated into its satire of the world of modern advertising.

Like Wimsey, Sayers also achieved a first at Oxford, in modern languages and medieval literature in her case. Unlike him, however, she had to wait some years for her degree to be awarded, women at Oxford not being permitted to take their degrees at the time. After not graduating, she joined a London advertising agency where she worked as a copywriter from 1922 to 1931. The first five Wimsey novels were published during these years, successfully enough for her to then cut free from the advertising world.

Her claim to fame as a copywriter was her Guinness Zoo advertisements, variations of which persisted for decades. A well-known example was that of a toucan with its bill arching into a glass of Guinness and a jingle by Sayers:

> If he can say as you can
> Guinness is good for you
> How grand to be a Toucan
> Just think what Toucan do

She is also believed to have coined the slogan 'It pays to advertise!' and in a different age might have come up with the catchphrase, 'Three Toucans Make a Six-Pack'.

Cricket is drawn directly into the world of advertising early in *Murder Must Advertise*. One of Wimsey's colleagues at Pym's Publicity, where he is working undercover using his middle names Death Bredon, consults him about googlies. Tomboy Toffee has embarked on a series of cricket advertisements beginning with 'Lumme, what a Lob!', followed by 'Yah! that's a Yorker!' and has reached the point when 'Gosh! it's a Googly' is to feature. Miss Meteyard wants to know what a googly is. Bredon demonstrates, first with pencil and paper and then out in the corridor with a small round tin of Good Judge tobacco. Tomboy Toffee eventually finishes its Cricket Campaign with the portraits of a complete Eleven of famous cricketers. Sadly, Sayers doesn't name them.

Sayers has fun with advertising – parts of the novel are like a genial version of *Mad Men* – but there are moments when her good-humoured satire deepens into a much darker treatment. There is an extraordinary set-piece when Bredon contemplates the world of advertising, a world which he, like other rich men, had never paid attention to because the wealthy can buy what they want. Advertising, on the other hand, is for the comparatively poor, for 'those who, aching for a luxury beyond their reach and for a leisure ever denied them, could be bullied or wheedled into spending their few hardly earned shillings on whatever might give them, if only for a moment, a leisured and luxurious illusion':

> Phantasmagoria – a city of dreadful day, of crude shapes and colours piled Babel-like in a heaven of harsh cobalt and rocking over a void of bankruptcy – a Cloud Cuckooland, peopled by pitiful ghosts, from the Thrifty Housewife providing a Grand Family Meal for Fourpence with the aid of Dairyfields Butter Beans in Margarine, to the Typist capturing the affections of Prince Charming by a liberal use of Muggins's Magnolia Face Cream.

In like manner, Tomboy Toffee aimed to feed the aspirations of ambitious young cricketers and sweeten the memories of those whose aspirations had turned to nostalgia. The novel concludes with another blistering set-piece:

> Tell England [that phrase again] […] Eat more Oats […] Shine your shoes with Shino […] Try Dogsbody's Sausages […] Flush your Kidneys with Fizzlets […] Popp's Pills Pep you Up […] Advertise, or go under' [the closing words of the novel].

Sayers knew her cricket fiction. Although the setting of her cricket match is distinctive, surely the first example in fiction of an office match between two companies, her debt to De Sélincourt and, to a lesser extent Macdonell, is clear. Disputes and recriminations over selecting the team and the proposed batting order dominate preparations for the game. Tallboy, the captain, omits Smayle because the previous year he'd turned out in 'white suede shoes with crocodile vamps and an incredible blazer with Old Borstalian colours'. When another member of the team falls off a step-ladder and breaks his leg, Tallboy is forced to eat humble pie and beg Smayle to play, with predictable results. The prickly pride, petty rancour and class resentments of office life, also reminiscent of any cricket club, threaten the declared purpose of the match to cultivate team and office spirit.

Pym's opponents are Brotherhood Ltd, a Romford company which manufactures boiled sweets and non-alcoholic liqueurs and is one of their major clients. It's a Saturday fixture, the team travels to the match in the office charabanc, and the rest of the office follow by the afternoon train to lend their support. Brotherhood's has its own cricket field and a crimson flag embroidered with their trademark of two clasped hands which also adorns their crimson blazers and caps. Pym's, by contrast, are 'a poor advertisement for themselves'. Bredon in faultless flannels and his Balliol blazer is their only bright spot. One of the team spoils his beautifully laundered outfit by wearing a brown felt hat, while others combine white flannels with brown shoes, tweed coats with white linen hats and grey flannel trousers with a striped shirt and braces. Although the setting is a far cry from the village grounds of De Sélincourt and Macdonell – Brotherhood's opening bowler comes in from the factory rather than the village pond end – many features of that world persist. Old Mr Brotherhood, a cheerfully doddering gentleman of 75 who comes each year to watch the match, is a figure from the earlier tradition, the aged onlooker with a deep memory who reminisces of all the cricket matches he's ever seen and tends to be avoided.

The match, a two-innings affair, begins promptly at 10:00, as befits a contest between two businesses. Brotherhood manages 155 in their first innings, and Pym's reply begins comfortably enough until Simmonds – 'a short, pugnacious-looking person with a scowl' – is brought on to bowl. The Brotherhood wicketkeeper 'hurriedly retires to a respectful distance'.

> The ferocious Simmonds wetted his fingers greedily, pulled his cap fiercely over his eyes, set his teeth in a snarl of hatred, charged like a bull and released the ball with the velocity of a 9-inch shell in Mr Barrow's direction.

But Simmonds, like Macdonell's blacksmith, is both fast and erratic. The ball pitches short, 'rockets up like a pheasant', whizzes past Mr Barrow's ear and is fielded by long-stop, a man with 'hands of leather'. Simmonds wreaks havoc, and Pym struggle through to 99. Bredon, coming in late in the order, is left not out on 14, having stuck to his plan to play quietly and unobtrusively. If he's to preserve his cover, there must be nothing to suggest Lord Peter Wimsey of 20 years ago making successive centuries for Oxford at Lord's.

The afternoon is oppressively hot, there's a threat of thunder and both teams are suffering from the generous glassfuls of gaseous Sparkling Pomagne, one of Brotherhood's non-alcoholic refreshers – 'made from finest Devon apples' – imbibed over lunch. Brotherhood can only manage 114 in their second innings, the single highlight of which is when their most dangerous batter is brilliantly run-out by a point-blank throw from the boundary. The fielders celebrate, old Mr Brotherhood cheers the speed and accuracy of the throw, but Bredon turns white and feels a little nauseous.

Pym's are left needing 171 to win, but their top order crumbles, and when Bredon comes to the wicket, they are 92 for 7. He's to face another example of that recurring figure in cricket fiction, a bowler with an outlandish action.

> He started his run from a point in the dim, blue distance, accelerated furiously to within a yard of the wicket, stopped, hopped, and with an action suggestive of a Catherine-wheel, delivered a medium-length, medium-paced, sound straight ball of uninspired but irreproachable accuracy.

Bowling actions offer so much more to the writer than the limited range of batting styles. With real-life models as eccentric as Douglas Wright, Paul Adams, the wrong-footed Max 'Tangles' Walker and Lance Cairns, and Jasprit Bumrah, they are a field of rich possibilities for the novelist.

Sayers, here, makes her own distinctive contribution. In the act of his first delivery to Bredon, 'round about the stop-and-hop period', her bowler loses his footing, performs 'a sort of splits', and is helped off the field. The demon Simmonds is brought back on. His third delivery spits up off the bumpy pitch and cannons into Bredon's elbow. It hurts, and Bredon, seeing red, is transformed into Wimsey: 'He forgot his caution and his role, and Mr Miller's braces, and saw only the green turf and the Oval on a sunny day and the squat majesty of the gasworks.' He 'opens his wrathful shoulders' to the next delivery, a bumper, and clears the leg-side boundary. And so it continues. Wimsey sees them home, winning the match with a six which 'soared away in a splendid parabola, struck the pavilion roof with a noise like the crack of doom, rattled down the galvanised iron roofing, bounced into the enclosure where the scorers were sitting and broke a bottle of lemonade'. Bredon returns to the pavilion 83 not out.

Old Mr Brotherhood is ecstatic. As he's earlier made clear, speaking with the voice of cricket and Henry Newbolt, he doesn't care who wins or loses 'provided they play the game'. And his long memory of cricket threatens to blow Wimsey's cover. 'Aren't you Wimsey of Balliol?' he asks, as he congratulates the hero on his beautifully played innings: 'I could have taken my oath that the last time I saw you play it was at Lord's in 1911, when you made 112'. Before Bredon is able to answer, several policemen and a detective approach and, having confirmed that he is Mr Death Bredon, arrest him on a charge of murder. Hence the title of the chapter: 'Unexpected Conclusion of a Cricket Match'.

Writing about a murder mystery presents a problem. How to discuss this novel, and the others to follow in the chapter, without revealing the answer to the mystery? Sayers's particular contribution to the genre is that the decisive clue to the murder, the run-out which leaves Pym's team celebrating and Bredon very disturbed, occurs in the course of the match itself. The death at the advertising agency which Wimsey is investigating involves a long-range shot from a catapult through a skylight, causing the victim to fall down a steep iron spiral staircase. The murderer, as Wimsey later discloses, would have to be a wonderfully good shot with a missile – 'the kind of man who could spread-eagle a wicket from the other end of a cricket field'. More than this I won't say, except that the denouement is more complicated than my bald summary suggests, and so too is Bredon's arrest.

Orwell said of Sayers that her stories, considered as detective stories, lacked 'the minimum of probability that even a detective story ought to have, and the crime is always committed in a way that is incredibly tortuous and quite uninteresting'. Mysteries are always more interesting than their solution, but Sayers's use of a run-out in *Murder Must Advertise* to help reveal the identity of the murderer is no more tortuous and certainly more ingenious than most.

The sun is low in the west. The game is over. The 145th fixture between the rival Surrey villages of Thames Pagnall and Maplecot – 47 victories each, 50 draws – has ended in a nail-biting tie. The appointment of neutral umpires (their fee: a guinea apiece plus tea and 2 pints) from a club twenty miles away has avoided the ill-feeling of the previous year over a disputed LBW decision. This year, the teams have retired amicably to the Green Man, and Old George Crombie, Thames Pagnall's grounds-man for the last 50 years, is trundling his handcart around the boundary collecting the deck chairs and folding stools. It's heavy work. Almost the whole village has turned out for the match. On the far side of the ground, he finds someone lying back in a deckchair, a grey trilby over their face, apparently asleep and unaware that the match is over. When Crombie tries to rouse him, there's no response. The man is dead, shot in the back. No one knows who he is, no one has noticed him at the game, no one has seen or heard anything suspicious, and there's nothing on the dead man to identify him.

This is the brilliant opening scene of E. & M. A. Radford's *Murder Isn't Cricket* (1946), the open-air version of a closed-room murder mystery that exploits the drama of an exciting finish to create a seemingly insoluble crime. What follows, however, doesn't live up to its early promise. Edwin and Mona Morgan were a husband-and-wife team who together published 38 mysteries between 1944 and 1972, all but three of them featuring Dr Harry Manson, a Chief Detective-Inspector of Scotland Yard and head of its Crime Research Laboratory. Edwin Morgan, a journalist, had been arts editor for the *Daily Mirror* before taking to crime writing, and Mona had been an actor in musical comedy and revues. Their writing practice, as described by Edwin, was: 'She kills them off, and I find out how she done it.'

If so, Mona was the more gifted of the two. Edwin's schtick was to high-light the scientific methods of investigation practised by Manson, which means the reader is subjected to long, turgid passages in which his detec-tive explains to the wonderment of his plodding colleagues how he's cal-culated the angle from which the bullet was fired by taking into account the shadow of the sun's decline at the estimated time of death, and so on and on. The last chapter, 'L'Envoi: The Seven Points', even lists and describes the seven vital clues that arose during Manson's investigation and which the reader and the rest of the police force are presumed to have overlooked.

The novel's original Crime Book Society cover featured a batter with a skull playing a front-foot drive, and a spine with a skull rather than bails on a set of wickets, but, in fact, cricket barely figures at all. Four possible suspects are found to have the unimpeachable alibi of having been playing in full view of the onlookers at the time of the murder, and otherwise, cricket as such falls out of sight. Apart that is from the guilty party being called Bosanquet [the inventor of the googly]. I've no hesitation in offering this spoiler because the reader, unlike Manson's police colleagues, will not be left gaping in astonishment at the final revelation.

The murdered man turns out to be an Australian detective who has tracked down a drug trafficker living in a house overlooking the Thames Pagnall cricket ground. Sayers had used a drug narrative in *Murder Must Advertise*, though not to her satisfaction. In the letter to Victor Gollancz I quoted from earlier she'd written: the novel 'deals with the dope-traffic, which is fashionable at the moment, but I don't feel this part is very convincing, as I can't say "I know dope"'. But in fact her treatment of the drug world of the 'bright young things' of the time is altogether more stylish and engaging than the Radfords's stiff-necked and censorious mocking of that same world. Sayers's description of a lavish costume party at the Richmond home of the head of her drug gang, where Wimsey, dressed in the black-and-white of a Harlequin costume, dives from the top of an elaborate statue-group of mermaids and dolphins into a fountain pool, is especially so.

It's hardly surprising that the cricket murder mystery of the mid-twentieth century should have migrated to public school cricket fiction. A school cricket ground offers a double setting for a murder mystery, an enclosed space within an enclosed space, with a large cast of potential suspects – staff, pupils, visiting parents – and an institution organised around strictly regulated hierarchies liable to provoke resentments and fuel thoughts of revenge among both those who teach and those who learn.

An early example was Nicholas Blake's *A Question of Proof* (1935) – the first of his 16 Nigel Strangeways mysteries – this one set in a prep school, Sudeley Hall. Blake was the pseudonym of the future Poet Laureate Cecil Day-Lewis, already well-known as a member of the circle of poets who had gathered around W. H. Auden at Oxford in the 1920s. After Oxford, he'd worked as a schoolmaster while publishing several highly regarded volumes of poetry, his *Collected Poems* (1935) having sealed his reputation. But neither poetry nor school teaching paid well, and *A Question of Proof* was very much a question of income. It sold over 200,000 copies and, together with its successors, enabled Day-Lewis from then on to live by his writing. He became Poet Laureate in 1968 and died four years later.

Nigel Strangeways is an amateur gentleman detective, the nephew of an assistant commissioner at Scotland Yard, and a not too distant relation of Lord Peter Wimsey. Originally, though, he was modelled on Day-Lewis's friend Auden and given several of that poet's distinguishing characteristics, in particular, a constant need for enormous quantities of tea, cigarettes and heaps of bedclothes. Eccentricity is the hallmark of the gentleman detective. Sitting up in bed 'under a mountain of blankets and eiderdowns', pondering the intricacies of the mystery he's working to solve, Strangeways's breakthrough is registered by his throwing back his head and extinguishing his cigarette on 'the topmost eiderdown'. Auden's friends would have got the joke. He was notorious for taking down the curtains from any room he happened to be staying in and tossing them on his bed, and even once, though the story must surely be apocryphal, adding an oil painting from the wall to the pile.

There are two murders in *A Question of Proof*. The first occurs early in the novel at the annual Sudeley Hall Sports Day while the onlookers are gripped by the close finish of an exciting 440 race. The second happens at the climax of the annual cricket match against the parents just as the school team hits the winning run. At the precise moment of victory, the headmaster, Percy Vale, who is sitting in a deckchair on the boundary, with his wife next to him and staff and parents alongside, slumps sideways to the ground with blood oozing through the back of his coat. He's been stabbed. No one among the 200 spectators has witnessed the murder, and there's no trace of the weapon even though the scene is instantly sealed off.

We have another example of an open-air closed-room murder committed while a crowd is absorbed in the dangerous pastime of watching a cricket match, especially if you're reclined in a deckchair. Blake, though, makes more interesting use of the possibilities of this setting than the Radfords, so I won't reveal the solution. As Strangeways explains, the murderer has worked on the same principle as the pickpocket: 'at moments of great excitement, everyone's attention is focused on one point and the whole strength of mass-emotion keeps it fixed on that point'. There is safety in numbers when committing murder in such a crowd because the culprit, although in plain sight, is invisible. And everyone has either 'a perfect alibi or no alibi at all', as the Police Superintendent, who is working a little resentfully with Strangeways on the crime, ruefully puts it. Blake exploits these factors to create the tension, the jeopardy and the mystery needed for a successful story of murder.

Murder during a cricket match, and at a public school of all places, feels instinctively wrong, almost an act of violence against England itself. While investigating the first murder, Strangeways has taken time out to watch a match between the school's first and second elevens, enjoying that mood of 'aesthetic rapture and expert attention which the cricket devotee shares only with the lover of music and the fisherman'. The seconds have been strengthened by the inclusion of several staff, and Strangeways is admiring the batting of the senior assistant master, Tiverton, one of his suspects for the sports day murder. The man is a born cricketer, he thinks: 'No man who could bat like that would commit a mean and cowardly murder'. Strangeways is momentarily held in a 'timeless trance of the sky, green grass and gracious action' in which cricket makes the very idea of murder seem impossible. This also makes it an ideal setting for one to occur.

Nancy Spain's murder novel *Death Before Wicket* (1946) is full of sport – horse racing, lacrosse, tennis and cricket – sports at which she herself was adept. Although she wrote in her frothy and unreliable memoir *Why I'm Not a Millionaire* (1956) that the only game she'd ever been any good at was cricket, in fact, she played lacrosse for the Northumberland and Durham county team, hockey for the North of England and was proficient at tennis and horse-riding. A well-known journalist and broadcaster (an early pan-ellist on 'My Word', 'What's My Line' and 'Juke Box Jury') she covered the last test of the 1953 Ashes series for the *Daily Express*. Spain died, aged 46, when a small plane taking her to Aintree to report on the 1964 Grand National crashed as it came in to land. It's an eerie coincidence that the closing page of her memoir involves a helicopter flight over London: 'the Thames [...] a beautifully painted river on an animated map [...] the green and tufty parks spread all below us, idle as a bedspread', making her wish for a helicopter of her own.

Death Before Wicket opens at a point-to-point race meeting somewhere in Yorkshire. The 'Ladies Race' is won by Joan Weir, a *femme fatale* and games mistress at the nearby school of St Anne Athaway's. She's wearing 'a pair of snow-white buckskin jodhpurs that fitted every dimple of her legs', and a cream camel-hair overcoat under which her royal blue racing silks shone. We next see her warming up for an exhibition match of lacrosse between England and the Rest at a famous girls' school in Brighton, based on Roedean where Spain had boarded in the early 1930s. Joan emerges from the pavilion running swiftly, catching and passing the ball at speed, dressed in navy blue and white, 'her black legs flashing against the green grass', looking 'like a young Greek sprinter'. A watching group of school-girls 'sigh ecstatically' as she dashes past.

We next see Joan back at St Anne Athaway's about to umpire the annual cricket match between the girls and their fathers. She's just put on her umpire's coat and is preparing to get the match started. A large crowd of staff, parents and children are milling around in front of the pavilion. Mrs Harrigon, the scorer, is sharpening her pencil with a razor. She cuts herself, blood starts from her finger and the other umpire springs forward to help her, blood staining her white coat. Joan turns 'a nasty greenish white' and faints. A smelling-bottle is produced. And then, 'Joan Weir's life went out, in suffocation and a slow convulsion; in rigidity, and above all, in a bitter, bitter smell of almonds'.

Death Before Wicket makes imaginative and witty play with the village and public school traditions of cricket writing. The epigraph comes from De Sélincourt's *The Cricket Match* – 'There was no denying the fact that people had been killed at cricket' – and subsequent epigraphs to the novel's four parts also nod to its predecessors. One is from Mary Russell Mitford's *Our Village* – 'Cricketers [...] are too important persons in our village to be talked of merely as figures in the landscape'; there's another from De Sélincourt; and intriguingly there's one from 'Prince Ranjitsinjhi': 'You should get your first hundred for the side, the next you should get for the side, and then you may get one for yourself'.

Spain is also very aware of the tradition of gentleman detectives and amateur sleuths in crime fiction. Early in the novel, we see the French teacher at Athaway's, Mlle Peugeot, sitting in the staff common room enjoying Ngaio Marsh's *Death in a White Tie* (1938). *Death Before Wicket* has an equivalent to Marsh's gentleman Scotland Yard detective, Roderick Alleyn, in the character of Mr Ingledew of Scotland Yard, one of the fathers playing in the match. More striking is her treatment of the fig-ure of the amateur sleuth. Johnny DuVivien is a complete break from the tradition of Raffles, Wimsey and Strangeways. He's an Australian former all-in wrestler, proprietor of the local Heeton Arms Roadhouse and of a West End club 'the bag of tricks'. Johnny is married to a former Russian ballet dancer, Natasha, and together they provide a gently satiric commentary on the customs and practices of the English with which the novel has much fun. Its concluding sentence is Natasha's – 'The English,' said Natasha, 'are a very strange lot' – and it is her indolent perspicacity, together with Johnny's energetic intelligence, that solves the mystery of Joan Weir's murder.

Despite Joan's murder, the headmistress decides that the afternoon, including the tea interval entertainment of 50 girls providing a Greek dancing display, should proceed as if nothing untoward has happened. Joan's body is taken into the pavilion, the doors are locked, a member of staff is left to guard the corpse and her death is kept under wraps. The game must proceed. Mrs Harrigon, the flow of blood from her finger now staunched, puts on Joan's white coat and the match begins.

Descriptions of the cricket alternate with scenes from around the boundary. The watching girls poke fun at both teams. Dennis Wynne, one of Jane Weir's several hapless suitors and still oblivious to her death, bowls to Mabel Moss:

> He pranced up to the wicket and tied himself into a confused knot of arms and legs. Then the ball flew out of his hand and rose and rose and rose in a fantastic lob. Mabel followed it most of the way, lost sight of it for a moment, swung her bat miserably, missed it and was bowled by what is known as a 'donkey drop'.

Another for the collection of eccentric actions and lobs scattered through cricket fiction. A group of girls on the bank chant: 'May-bell Moss / Bowled by a Full-Toss'.

Mr Ingelow, informed of the death, has agreed that the afternoon should continue as planned, at least until the county police and photographers from the Yard arrive. But Cecilia Harrigon, daughter of the replacement umpire, who has a heavy crush on Miss Weir, climbs through the rear window of the pavilion to find out what's happened to her idol, discovers the corpse and rushes outside screaming. The cat is out of the bag. A crowd gathers, the cricket is adjourned and the dancers are called on to provide some distraction. Miss Jones, megaphone in hand, 'the frills and furbelows of her Ascot gown frothing and swaying' as she makes her way out onto the ground, assembles the troupe of 50 dancers (including the cricket team) all clad in unbecoming garments of yellow butter muslin. The band strikes 'raggedly' into Schubert's 'Rosamunde' and Natasha, weeping with laughter, collapses ecstatically into a deckchair: 'Like cows in a bog!' she splutters.

Death Before Wicket is a *jeu d'esprit* which draws on Spain's own school years. In *Why I'm Not a Millionaire*, she described the Roedean anthem, 'The

Cricket First Eleven', roared out by the great body of Old Roedeanians who would rush each year to the school 'like lemmings' for the annual cricket match against the girls. Some would even change into their old djibbahs – a garment 'rather like a sack' – which was compulsory uniform at Roedean until 1935 when, to the disgust of generations of Old Roedeanians, it was abolished. 'The Cricket First Eleven' was sung to the tune of the South African War song, 'Tommy, Tommy Atkins':

O, the Cricket First Eleven
Is the best in all the land.
It's the one above all others
We admire on every hand.
May your scores be never-failing
And your bowling ever true.
O, noble First eleven
Here's our best of healths to you.

When Spain sang this to her close friend Noel Coward, he cried with mirth, added the song to his cabaret act and performed it in Las Vegas.

Spain's writing in *Death at the Wicket* is brisk, witty and stylish, its succinct character descriptions brilliant: one of the staff, Miss Practice (her name a clever double pun), has 'teeth that resembled letters protruding through the letter-box of a pale front door'; Admiral Piper is 'a little pink robin of a man'; Major Rubens looks like 'a small purple eagle with a white moustache'; Mrs Harrigon's glance 'appeared full of broken glass and corkscrews'. The description of a 'massive member of the Yorkshire Constabulary' (nothing in this novel is innocent) getting to his feet is Dickensian: 'He seemed to straighten himself in sections.' Cricket is treated affectionately but without respect; public schools with neither. When Major Rubens says to Johnny: 'Damn it, sir [...] Murders don't happen every day in girls' schools, do they?', Natasha responds, 'I have often been wondering why not'. A comic cricket murder mystery with touches of pain and loss, *Death at the Wicket* is a one-off.

It's late afternoon and the heat and glare of the sun is beginning to subside. Tea has been taken, the village side is about to start its run-chase, and the Squire, Pierce Elliot, is leading his team onto the field.

The Squire moved benignly with his men into the midst of this fading, quiet arena. To Randall his presence made it again a charmed space, an isolated piece of England with the vast, loud, dangerous world outside shut off for an hour or two longer [...] Randall caught himself wishing, not for the first time, that it might go on for ever.

Randall is the village doctor whose uncharacteristically dogged innings has helped carry the Squire's team to a total of 202. The reason for his painfully slow innings of carefully accumulated singles, while avoiding the strike as much as possible, will be revealed later in the novel.

Barbara Worsley-Gough's *Alibi Innings* (1954) was published a year after *The Go-Between* and bears a superficial resemblance to Hartley's novel. Although set in present time, it could just as easily be 1900. When the Squire walks out to bat, he's wearing his I.Z. cap as if he's going out to join Raffles at the crease. His I.Z. blazer, aired on a lavender hedge the previous day to get rid of the smell of mothballs, is also part of his garb for the day. This enduring figure, 'the guardian angel of village cricket' as the novel describes him, represents a paternalistic and deferential social world reaching back to the nineteenth century, one which the novel accepts without question. The village side is left mainly voiceless and when one of its players, Bill Bird, a Council roadman and 'its dullest witted member', speaks, the effect is toe-curling: 'Thinks 'e'll get me caught by 't young 'un behind the wicket, does 'e? Roight, let 'un troy, then.'

But in other respects, it's not at all a bad novel. One of its virtues is the inventive way it incorporates cricket into the murder rather than merely using it as a backdrop. Its opening scene has familiar echoes; only this time, it's not a young-un excited by the prospect of a cricket match but a 69-year-old squire.

> The annual cricket match between the Squire's eleven and the village side was the happiest event of the year for him. He looked forward to it eagerly for six months, and enjoyed it critically in retrospect for six months afterwards.

It's the morning of the match and the team is gathering on the terrace of his Queen Anne house. Several of them – a friend of his late son, his grandson and a couple of his friends – have come down from London. The rest are local gentry, including the rector, of course, and, as the social exception proving the class rule, the gardener of the Squire's extensive estate. The terrace overlooks the Squire's cricket ground, but he prefers his guests to form a party and watch play from the boundary, a little apart from but adjacent to the gathered villagers. The only fly in the ointment is Elizabeth Elliot, the squire's wife – 'a wiry, well-preserved, disagreeable woman with a large income and a great many enemies' – who loathes cricket. She's the author of 51 novels, their titles all taken from Shakespeare.

The description of the match is flat and derivative. There's an erratic fast bowler whom Worsley-Gough neglects to provide with an occupation. The blacksmith must have been a disappearing figure by the 1950s. A lofted drive results in mid-on and long-on colliding as they run to take the catch. A striker loses his bat and his balance and sits on his wicket. The bat sails through the air and bludgeons cover-point. There's none of the brio and anarchic humour of Macdonell.

But the cricket is nicely integrated with the novel's theme of marriage. It's a bit like Jane Austen with cricket, as the pressure of the match and other events of the day lead to the break-up of several engagements and the restoration of previously abandoned ones. Jane Austen, I'm reminded, was no stranger to cricket. In *Northanger Abbey* her young heroine, Catherine Morland, much prefers it to books, and Austen's family was full of cricketers, five of whom rated an obituary in *Wisden*.

One of the engagements that unravels is that of Mrs Elliot's niece, Anthea, and a young man from London, Oliver Firth. The treatment of Firth is interesting but unfortunate. He's tall, elegant, with dark hair and eyes and a languid manner which causes others to wonder if he has 'Indian blood in him'. The chief constable describes him as having a 'dagoish charm'. Firth has a flat in the Albany 'which he shares with a friend by the name of Bruce', and is involved in the disappearance of a brooch of Mrs Elliot's, an unmistakable echo of Raffles.

But, in a similar manner to Austen's novels, the dysfunctional marriages we see cast a potential shadow on those being made. Think, for example, of the Bennets in *Pride and Prejudice*. We learn about the Squire's miserable marriage on the opening page of *Alibi Innings*:

> The squire had learned long ago to control his anger because he lived with a tyrant. He had become very patient and gentle as a result of trying successfully for many years not to hate his wife. He did not like her because that was more than flesh and blood could compass, but he did still love her a little, out of Christian charity and a strong sense of fitness and because he had almost no one else to love.

After seeing Mrs Elliot conversing waspishly with the squire's guests on the terrace before retreating to her study as the squire and his team prepare for the match, it's little surprise that later in the afternoon she's found dead, her head slumped forward on her desk, 'her elaborately arranged white hair [...] covered with blood'. It's easy to spot the victim from early on.

No one is sorry about her murder. One of the characters describes how awful it is when somebody you've known all your life is dead and you aren't sorry. On the night of his wife's murder, the squire falls asleep within a few minutes of going to bed and begins 'to dream almost at once of an endless and idyllic cricket match'. There's no suggestion of criticism here. It's almost as if someone who so hated cricket deserves to be murdered. But it's more than that too. The novel's treatment of love and death is serious and its use of cricket to explore these matters is distinctive. *Alibi Innings*, though socially conservative and sometimes worse, is psychologically and emotionally involving, and the cricket match is central to this.

But there's no avoiding its complacent endorsement of a social world dating back to Victorian and Edwardian times. Hartley, looking back half a century, shows the world of the big house and the village beginning to crumble. *The Go-Between* ends in disorder and, despite the sadness and regrets of its two main characters, the society we have seen at work and play in its retrospective narrative is not mourned. *Alibi Innings*, on the other hand, ends with the restoration of order. As the squire falls contentedly asleep, the world is just as it was and forever should be. Cricket is its own alibi.

A feature common to all cricket mystery writing is that murder must never stop the game from proceeding. The solution of the murder in *Alibi Innings* is inventive and would be a shame to reveal, but it spoils little to know that one of the squire's team has actually discovered the body of Mrs Elliot just before the match is to begin but has said nothing because, as always, the game must go on. This is also true of Ted Dexter and Clifford Makins' maladroit cricket murder novel, *Testkill* (1976), a title that sounds like a pesticide and a story with as many loose ends as an upturned knitting bag. On the opening day of an Ashes test at Lord's, an Australian fast bowler drops dead in his delivery stride. Poison is suspected and confirmed. On the third evening of the test, a distinguished cricket journalist is killed in a hit-and-run job, and the narrator, a former international cricketer, survives a brutal attack with a cricket bat. The next morning, the president of the MCC is murdered. But the match, nevertheless, proceeds laboriously to its conclusion. It's quite an achievement that such mayhem should be wholly devoid of drama. *Testkill* is the nadir of the cricket murder mystery novel and possibly of all cricket fiction.

Since then, television rather than the novel has become the more frequent medium for the cricket murder. The Inspector Morse episode 'Deceived by Flight' (3:3, 1989) uses many of the tropes and conventions of the novel genre. An old college roommate of Morse's, Anthony Donn, has come to Oxford for the annual fixture against his old college and is found murdered in his room. Again, this is no reason to postpone the match. As his old college coach insists – 'The Festival will continue'.

Cricket permeates the episode. It opens with Morse in his office listening to a Saint-Saens Cello Concerto. The piece ends and the radio goes over to Lord's, where England is playing [...] we never learn who, because Morse abruptly switches off the broadcast in disgust. Lewis, his assistant, wants to know the score and is sharply put in his place. But the cricket commentary is on everywhere: in the college porters' lodge, in the bedroom where Donn is unpacking just before he dies and where Lewis begins to investigate his murder. We hear the voice of Brian Johnston describing the curious 'hop-skip run-up' of the bowler (a clever nod to the genre) and the batter being 'deceived by the flight' and stumped. The commentary is like a soundtrack, a score, to the unfolding story.

Colin Dexter, the progenitor of Morse, Lewis and Endeavour, had the idea for this episode after learning that Kevin Whately, who plays Lewis, loved cricket and had once hoped to play the game professionally. Dexter himself, Colin that is, not Ted, also confessed that his unfulfilled ambition was to open the batting for England. Lewis goes undercover as a college porter and is recruited into the college team as he pursues his investigation. He's running in to bowl, having just taken a wicket when there's a scream from the pavilion as a second body is discovered. The most likely suspects for the murder of Donn are all out on the pitch. As with other cricket murder stories, the match itself appears to provide the guilty party with a water-tight alibi.

The mystery and its resolution are too complex to summarise, and too dexterous to attempt to do so, but as with the best of such writing, cricket is more than just a setting for murder. When Morse, watching the match as part of his inquiries, is asked if he follows cricket, he replies that he normally flees it: 'Men in uniform, incomprehensible rules, nothing happening for hours on end', he remarks. Morse, the disillusioned idealist, will always find art more rewarding than life, except it seems for the art of cricket and, from the discarded book at his feet, the art of motorcycle maintenance.

The cricket murder mystery has also seeped into cosy crime television drama, even so far as Death in Paradise (6:4, 2017). Two episodes of Midsomer Murders, however – 'Dead Man's Eleven' (2:3, 1999) and 'Last Man Out' (19:3, 2017) – stand out. Both repeat the trope of the police detective turning undercover cricketer to investigate a murder. 'Dead Man's Eleven' opens with a cricket match on a village green and a character (played by Imelda Staunton) remarking that 'If Jesus had played a sport it would have been cricket', an assertion the episode sets out to disprove. It has two murders, the first committed with a cricket bat on the edge of a quarry, the second with a Nazi war knife in the score-box as a game between Midsomer Worthy and Fletcher's Cross is being played. Once again, cricket offers good cover for a murder because everyone's attention is fixed on the game. But here it also provides a vital clue. An error in the scoring – a single rather than a boundary is put up on the board – leads Barnaby to discover what must really have happened.

In 'Last Man Out', two murders and an attempted one all employ cricket gear. The first is ingenious and rather horrifying, with the captain of Lower Pampling Panthers being killed by a volley of cricket balls fired at high velocity from the club's bowling machine. The second involves a cricket stump being fired into the back of the new captain by a jealous rival. The attempted murder, more conventionally, employs a cricket bat, but unconventionally it is wielded by a former England women's cricket captain.

This later episode of Midsomer Murders breaks with several aspects of the cricket murder mystery and, indeed, the traditional culture of the English village game itself. There's a nod to ethnic diversity, a recent feature of the series, but it is cricket itself that we see in the process of transformation. C-10, a ten-overs competition imported from Australia, has been introduced to the world of Midsomer. This has so divided the inhabitants of Lower Pampling that a referendum on whether it should continue is being held. The very existence of the village game, indeed English culture itself, is at stake. The traditionalists are led by the ex-England women's cricket captain. Most of the players are on the side of the innovators and don't at all mind being rebranded as the Panthers, but they are unaware that C-10 is being used as cover for a betting and match-fixing scam. Once more, a police detective goes undercover as a cricketer to investigate, but the crime he now solves is not just murder but also match-fixing.

Chapter 4

CRICKET AND COMEDY

Cynthia Hetherington said that cricket was the funniest game of all to watch [...] George, who was always a good host, refrained from saying that cricket was in no sense of the term a funny game at all: it was a great game, and exciting and dramatic and even at times tragic – but funny it emphatically was not.

–J. C. Masterman, *Fate Cannot Harm Me*

At Easter 1966, I was playing at the University Oval in Dunedin, now a test venue, in the national inter-university cricket tournament. My stumps had just been demolished by a tall, gangling, long-haired bowler, all knees and elbows, who'd let fire the quickest delivery I'd ever failed to see. My replacement had immediately gone the same way, and there was panic in the grandstand as the next batter, our wicketkeeper Don Cook, scrambled for his pads, box and gloves, stubbed out his cigarette and stumbled down the wooden steps of the pavilion where our team was sitting. I paused unbuckling my pads to watch him face the hat-trick ball, another thunderbolt that exploded into his thigh like an Exocet. None of us wore thigh pads, of course, but rather than nursing his injured limb, Don started to leap around as if he'd been attacked by a swarm of wasps, beating at his thigh and then struggling to pull down his trousers as a faint cloud of smoke gathered around him. The ball had thundered into his pocket and ignited the box of matches he'd left there in his haste to get to the wicket. As we fell about laughing, one of our team had the wit to gather the fire extinguisher from the back of the old wooden stand and rush with it out onto the ground. The bowler was Murray Webb, who was to have an all-too-brief first-class and international career (New Zealand Player of the Year 1973–1974 with 40 wickets in a five-match season at an average of 8) before becoming one of New Zealand's finest cartoonists and caricaturists.

This episode, I like to think, must have been one of the seeds of his later career.

Cricket, perhaps more than any other sport, lends itself to mishap and slapstick. Indeed, there's something intrinsically comic about a game that can run for five days without a result and which once, in a test between South Africa and England in 1939 – the 'timeless test' as it's known – was abandoned after 12 days of rain-interrupted play with England needing just 41 runs to win because the boat to take the team home was about to leave. There's also something rather comic about a game in which the box was introduced a century before the helmet and which is impossible to explain to anyone who hasn't been raised to understand it. Cricket is also a sport that has greatly appealed to dramatists – J. M. Barrie, Samuel Beckett, Harold Pinter, Tom Stoppard, Simon Gray, Alan Ayckbourn, David Hare, for example – but which is almost impossible to stage. Except that as I write, Shomit Dutta's play *Stumped*, in which Beckett and Pinter sit padded up waiting to go out to bat, has come online. The play was filmed at Lord's, no less. Cricket and the absurd have had a long partnership.

The complexity and confusion of cricket can begin long before the players have made their way onto the field. In a time before GPS, losing your way in finding the ground along narrow winding country lanes when, as often happened in Kent at least, the sign-posts had been swivelled around to point in the wrong direction. And then the dressing room, the territoriality and stink as 11 players and their coffin-sized cricket bags (the main source of the stink) squeeze into a space little bigger than a telephone box, and the anguished discovery that some crucial piece of gear is missing. 'Mum's forgotten to pack my socks', I remember a teammate in his late twenties exclaiming.

There is also the broader human comedy of the game, its mix of camaraderie and personal rivalry, nerves and swagger, team spirit and pettiness, of teenagers playing alongside septuagenarians, and the competing claims of the wicket and the hearth as 11 players bond over long afternoons and evenings, ignoring the call of love or duty, fashioning their excuses to justify their truancy.

It's no surprise, therefore, that a game so many writers have taken so very seriously – 'the greatest thing that God created on earth' according to Harold Pinter, 'an idea of the gods' as J. M. Barrie wrote – should so frequently have turned comic when they came to write about it. Foremost among these was P. G. Wodehouse, no mean cricketer. In his last two years at Dulwich College, 1899 and 1900, he opened the bowling for the School XI with N. A. Knox, a future England fast bowler, and his 7 for 50 against Tonbridge included the wicket of Kenneth Hutchings, who was also to play for England. Hugh De Sélincourt, described in the Dulwich school magazine as a promising leg-break bowler and useful batter, was another teammate of Wodehouse's at this time. After leaving Dulwich and reluctantly joining the Hong Kong and Shanghai Bank, Wodehouse played regularly in London bank cricket, an organised series of games played at well-appointed grounds in the outer suburbs that all the major banks had established at this period.

Wodehouse's time at the Hong Kong and Shanghai was short-lived, ending soon after 13 August 1902, on which day he had to leave the Oval at lunch and return to work, thereby missing most of Jessop's famous 76-ball century that took England to an unlikely victory over the Australians. Enough was enough, thought Wodehouse, and within a month he'd resigned. His cricket for the next few years was played among the many informal clubs and invitation elevens, which were a feature of the game in the Edwardian period, teams such as Barrie's Allahakbarries, the *Punch* XI and the Authors. These teams, drawing on a network of writer-cricketers including Conan Doyle, Hornung, A. A. Milne and De Sélincourt, enabled Wodehouse to play at Lord's on six occasions. On the last but one of these, playing for the Authors against the Publishers in 1911, he took 4 wickets and scored 60. More informally, men such as these would sometimes just organise a fixture and assemble an invitation XI. Wodehouse himself did this, taking a team back to his old school for five consecutive years from 1904 to 1908.

Wodehouse had left the bank not just to avoid having his cricket watching interrupted by a job, but to become a full-time writer, at which he proved extraordinarily prolific. Between 1902 and 1909, he wrote eight novels, most of them forgettable, as he later conceded, as well as short fiction for a number of periodicals. Some of these stories were about cricket.

'Reginald's Record Knock', written in 1909, opens with hints of the mature style that became Wodehouse's signature in his Blandings and Bertie Wooster novels: 'Reginald Humby was one of those men who go in just above the byes, and are to tired bowlers what the dew is to parched earth at the close of an August afternoon.' Light as a feather, sharp of wit and the playful use of cliché. The team Reginald plays for, the Hearty

Lunchers, epitomises the weekend away-club so typical of the period and a staple of cricket fiction at this time:

> Inveterate free-drinkers to a man, they wander about the country playing villages. They belong to the school of thought which holds that the beauty of cricket is that, above all other games, it offers such magnificent opportunities for a long drink and a smoke in the shade.

Reginald is 'a confirmed bat-oiler'. We first see him at home oiling his bat, almost certainly to no purpose, his manner at the crease being 'a sort of cross between hop-scotch, diabolo, and a man with gout in one leg trying to dance the Salome Dance'. His highest-ever score of 9 not out had been made in a house match at his prep school. But the Hearty Lunchers all love Reginald, and not just because he's 'one of those noble natures which are always good for five shillings'. He is the best of chaps.

This coming weekend, however, Reginald has been enlisted to play for the opposing team, Chigley Heath, the village where his fiancée, Margaret, lives. Learning of this, the captain of the Hearty Lunchers arranges for Reginald to be allowed to score a century in front of the watching Margaret. None of the Hearty Lunchers' regular bowlers will be used, and it's agreed that Reginald will open the batting. It's worth noting, perhaps, that 'batting for the other side' at this time also implied homosexuality, and 'to bat for both sides' was code for bisexuality. It's impossible to know whether or not Wodehouse's cherubic poker face and weightless writing style was innocent of these associations.

Wodehouse describes in detail the fastidious manner in which Reginald takes guard: tilting his cap, slowly marking two legs with a bail, surveying the field, patting down a blade of grass, fussily waving away two small boys from behind the bowler's arm, before eventually settling himself to receive the first ball, 'left toe well in the air'. This final detail, so typical of Wodehouse in its gently comic deflation of harmless pretension, is delicious. And typical of cricket too. I've noticed myself how the weakest of batters can be the most elaborate in preparing to face their first delivery, as if to prolong what will inevitably be a short stay at the crease.

But the joke is even better than I'd realised until I came across Conan Doyle's description of W. G. Grace's stance at the wicket. As the bowler approached, Doyle wrote in his obituary of Grace for *The Times*, 'he would slowly raise himself to his height, and draw back the blade of his bat, while his left toe would go upwards until only the heel of that foot remained upon the ground'. Reginald is imagining himself as W. G. Grace.

Assisted by the generosity of bowlers and fielders, Reginald, for the first time in his life, finds himself well set. The average batter, as Wodehouse remarks, has no idea of the whirl of sensations experienced by the really incompetent cricketer when for once in their life they notch a few:

> A wild exhilaration surges through him, followed by a sort of awe as if he were doing something wrong, even irreligious. Then all these yeasty emotions subside and are blended into one glorious sensation of grandeur and majesty, as of a giant among pygmies. This last state of mind does not come till the batsman's score has passed thirty.

Even the averagely competent batter for whom passing thirty is more common will recognise how Reginald feels as he waits contentedly for the ball to be retrieved from the boundary – 'that this was Life, that till now he had been a mere mollusc'.

Margaret has been prevented from attending the match but has arranged to meet Reginald at Brown's boathouse, a mile away from the ground, at 4:30. Suddenly, he notices the clock on the church tower. It's 4:15. What to do when, for the first time in his life, 'the ball seemed larger […] than a rather undersized marble'. His mind is quickly made up: 'What is Love compared to a chance of […] a really big score'? As Reginald reaches his century, the church clock, 'like a cold douche', strikes 6:00.

Reginald races to Margaret's house where the reception is decidedly frosty. But the day is saved when, confessing to his century, it transpires that Margaret loves cricket, plays regularly in ladies' matches and quite understands you can't abandon an innings in full flow. Each had mistakenly thought that poetry was the great love of the other and had kept their strong preference for cricket a secret. Romance and cricket are reconciled.

It almost never rains in Wodehouse's fictional world, but when, in another of his cricket short stories, it does, the result is a happy one. 'Between the Innings' is set during the annual cricket week at Heath Hall. Zingari and The Band of Brothers have already been defeated, and if the home team beats the Incogniti as well, it will be the first time it has ever gone through cricket week undefeated. The match is a two-day fixture. On the first day, the Hall has scored 250, the Incogs replied with 223, and at stumps, the Hall are 130 for 7. Overnight, the home team prays for rain. Their spin bowler, who is the narrator, is unplayable on a sticky wicket.

It's an oppressively hot night; summer lightning flickers, but the rain doesn't come. The narrator wanders out onto the ground, sits down by the pitch and lights a pipe. Suddenly, out of the darkness, he hears the sound of slopping water and discovers the young daughter of the Hall with a watering can. He persuades Ella, with whom he's in love, to abandon her pitch-tampering, and as she hands over the can, the rain arrives. We're left to assume that the next day brings victory to the Hall.

The story is slight and lacks the wit of 'Reginald's Record Knock', but it echoes that story and anticipates several others in having a young woman actively involved in the outcome of a match. 'Ladies and Gentleman v Players', for example, begins: 'Quite without meaning it, I really won the Gentleman v. Players match the summer I was eighteen'. The narrator is Joan Romney, who figures in several other Wodehouse stories in which her understanding of cricket enables her to sway the result of a game.

There's an under-remarked amount of short fiction about women's cricket in this period. J. M. Barrie's 'Ladies at Cricket' was first published in his collection of occasional pieces, *The Greenwood Hat* (1930), but dates back to early in the century. The narrator lies under a cherry tree watching a match between a ladies' school and eleven young women of the neighbourhood. The tone is comic but not disparaging and hardly at all condescending, very much in the mode of many stories of men's village cricket. The teams are described as 'flitting and darting in print and flannel', with a differently coloured rose at their waists. The winning side will take their opponent's roses. There's a mid-pitch collision between two 'batswomen' resulting in a run-out, and another dismissal when the bails are knocked off by the skirt of a batter's dress. There's a variety of bowling styles: 'swift daisy-cutters', 'overhand lobs' of course and one who bowls so quickly that the slips flee. The player of the match is 'Mary dear', a great hitter of the ball and such a good fielder that her team leaves all the catching to her. At one point in her innings, she becomes so excited at her dominance of the bowling that she even attempts to catch herself. Mary is a schoolmarm and mother of two.

Wodehouse's public school cricket novel *Mike* (1909) grew from a serial and was republished in 1953 as two separate novels, *Mike at Wrykin* and *Mike and Psmith*. The first of these, apart from the descriptions of cricket, is a tame affair. The writing is breezy but lacks the deft touch of Wodehouse's subsequent work; the rags and larks are predictable, and the tensions and jeopardies are obvious and uninvolving. Like the other school tales Wodehouse had been churning out since leaving Hong Kong and Shanghai, it was very much in the BOP tradition.

Mike and Psmith, however, marks the transition, as Benny Green described it, from 'juvenilia to the mature moonshine of vintage Wodehouse'. This comes with the introduction of Psmith (the 'P' is silent), 'a very long thin youth, with a solemn face [...] immaculate clothes [and] an eyeglass attached to a cord fixed in his right eye'. In style and manner, he's like an agreeable and witty version of Jacob Rees-Mogg, if such can be imagined. Like Mike, he has been 'superannuated', as he puts it, from a great cricketing public school, Eton in his case, and sent to Sedleigh, a very minor public school with no cricketing tradition whatsoever. Unlike Mike, however, he has taken this in his long, leisurely stride. With a typically Wildean flourish, he declares: 'Cricket I dislike, but watching cricket is one of the finest of Britain's manly sports'.

Mike, though, comes from a famous family of cricketers. Three of his older brothers play first-class cricket, one of them plays for England, and Mike, although only 15, promises to be the best of them all. He's already had three years in the Eleven of his famous cricketing school, Wrykin, and was about to become its captain when his father had him removed for gross academic idleness. *Raffles* is the only book Mike has ever read. At Sedleigh, he sulks in his tent, refusing to come out for cricket until late in the novel when he relents and, with the assistance of Psmith, now revealed as a subtle 'slow left-hand bowler with a curve', leads his new team to victory against his old school.

Wodehouse considered the second Mike story his best book, and George Orwell agreed with him. Alec Waugh was another admirer, describing it as 'the only great cricket story of recent times'. Waugh and Orwell, disaffected ex-public schoolboys themselves, would both have enjoyed the mockery of public school life and its fiction that Psmith gives casually eloquent voice to, but it's the cricket that Waugh singled out and that Wodehouse himself was most satisfied with, feeling, as he said, that he'd captured the 'ring of a ball on a cricket bat, the green of the pitch, the white of the flannels, the cheers of the crowd'.

The cricket in these two novels has many of the contemporary details one has come to expect. One of the MCC team that comes to play Wrykin is wearing a Zingari blazer. Scarves adorn waists. Lobs are 'the most dangerous, insinuating things in the world', and there are more eccentric bowling actions, with a particularly choice example in *Mike and Psmith*:

Mr Downing [...] took two short steps, two long steps, gave a jump, took three more short steps, and ended with a combination of step and jump, during which the ball emerged from behind his back and started on its slow career to the wicket. The whole business had some of the dignity of the old-fashioned minuet, subtly blended with the careless vigour of a cake-walk. The ball, when delivered, was billed to break from leg, but the programme was subject to alterations.

Wodehouse liked to incorporate real-life Test cricketers into his fiction. 'Ladies and Gentlemen v Players' includes three England test captains – C. B. Fry, F. S. Jackson and Archie MacLaren, as well as Wodehouse's Dulwich bowling partner N. A. Knox. He repeated this habit in *Mike* and updated it when the single novel became two in 1953. Fry, Hayward, Tyldesley and Rhodes regenerate as May, Sheppard, Compton and Hutton, and Knox returns as Trueman. But the cricketer whose name best lived on in Wodehouse's writing is his most famous character, Jeeves, the faultlessly assured and omni-competent manservant of Bertie Wooster. Percy Jeeves had a short but highly successful career as an all-rounder playing for Gloucester immediately before the First World War. Wodehouse had seen him playing at Edgbaston in 1913 and the name stuck in his mind, first appearing in his writing in 1916, just a few weeks after Percy Jeeves was killed in action in France.

Wodehouse was not the only writer-cricketer at the time to name his leading character after a professional cricketer. Legend has it that Conan Doyle derived Sherlock from the name of a Nottingham fast bowler Shacklock, and that of Holmes's brother Mycroft from a Derbyshire cricketer, William Mycroft. Doyle was one of Wodehouse's great heroes. It's reckoned that he mentioned Sherlock Holmes more than five hundred times in his writing, and when Holmes was resurrected from the Reichenbach Falls, Wodehouse welcomed him back with a poem of sorts in *Punch*:

'For we thought a wicked party
Of the name of Moriarty
Had dispatched him
[...]
But the very latest news is
That he merely got some bruises

[…]
It seems he wasn't hurt at all
By tumbling down the waterfall'

Doyle was 22 years older than Wodehouse, but they played cricket together on a number of occasions, sometimes for the Allahakbarries and once at Lord's when they opened the batting for the Authors against the Actors. Neither man had a good day, Wodehouse being dismissed for a duck and his partner for two.

Doyle, however, was a very competent cricketer. He played 10 first-class matches for the MCC, scoring 231 runs at an average of 19.25 and taking just 1 wicket for 50 runs. The wicket, however, was that of W. G. Grace for the MCC against London County at Crystal Palace in 1900, off a short delivery which Grace skied in attempting to hit out of the ground. The result was described in a poem Doyle wrote to celebrate the occasion, 'A Reminiscence of Cricket':

'Up, up like a towering game bird,
Up, up to a speck in the blue,
And then coming down like the same bird,
Dead straight on the line that it flew.

Good Lord, it was mine! Such a soarer
Would call for a pair of safe hands;
None safer than Derbyshire Storer,
And there, face uplifted, he stands.

Wicket keep Storer, the knowing,
Wary and steady of nerve,
Watching it falling and growing
Marking the pace and the curve.

I stood with my two eyes fixed on it,
Paralysed, helpless, inert;
There was "plunk" as the gloves shut upon it,
And he cuddled it up to his shirt.'

And so Grace – 'Walking he rumbled and grumbled' – departed the wicket.

Doyle wrote two cricket stories. The first of these – 'Three of Them II: About Cricket' published in *Strand Magazine* in 1918 – is a slightly embarrassing one in which a father reminisces about cricket with his two little boys at bedtime, rambling on with memories of how W. G. Grace (who Daddy has played against) would take guard with his left toe cocked in the air.

The other, 'The Story of Spedegue's Dropper' (1928), is more interesting. An old county cricketer, Walter Scougall, reckoned one of the best judges of the game, is walking in the New Forest when he comes upon a curious scene. A cord at least fifty feet above the ground has been strung up in a clearing between two large oaks. Cricket stumps have been placed on either side of the cord, the distance of a cricket pitch apart. A tall, thin young man is bowling lobs over the cord to a lad in wicketkeeping gloves. Scougall realises that what at first seems pure lunacy is in fact a perfectly targeted delivery, bowled with a leg-break action to swerve in the air, coming down with impeccable accuracy onto the bails or into the wicketkeeper's hands. The bowler, Spedegue, explains that if the ball is tossed high enough it develops pace as it falls, so that it's like facing a fast bowler from above. He describes the field that such a delivery requires: a packed leg-side with three on the boundary, a mid-on, two square, one fine and a rover. Scougall encourages him to put his idea into practice, which he does with great success, first in a village game, then in a house-party match between a local landowner's team and the Free Foresters.

Meanwhile, the England Selection Committee is deliberating over the team for the deciding test of the Ashes series. 'If only we could give them something new', one of the panel exclaims; the Australians 'have played every county and sampled everything we have got'. Another of the panel remembers a letter he's had from Scougall describing the strange technique and startling success of Spedegue. In the desperate hope that 'old Scougie' might have uncovered another Bosanquet and hasn't just been spending too much time out in the sun, they summon Spedegue for a secret trial: 'Lords at dawn'. They like what they see and decide to include him in the deciding test.

England bats first and scores 432. Spedegue is dismissed for a duck. Brought on to bowl at the start of the Australian innings, his first over is a disaster. He loses his nerve and sends down a succession of ordinary full-tosses which are severely punished. When, in desperation, he tries to imagine himself back in the New Forest, the ball soars fifty feet over the head of the wicketkeeper and to general hilarity is called a wide. But after taking an instinctive catch at 'fine slip', his nerves vanish and he finds his length. Every delivery now comes down on the top of the stumps. One of the Australians hits across the line of the fall and is bowled. Another knocks down his off-stump in trying to make contact. Catches are skied into the crowded leg-side field. Australia is dismissed for 71 and Spedegue has taken 7 for 31.

The follow-on innings follows suit. The star of the Australian batters adapts to these strange deliveries by improvising a back drive, turning and tapping the ball over the keeper's head, but the others are so trapped within orthodox methods of batting they are helpless: 'How could you play with a straight bat at a ball that fell from the clouds'? Spedegue finishes with 8 for 61, England win by an innings and 184 runs and the Ashes are secured.

The English are amused as much as exultant. The Australians are resentful at first but come to appreciate the absurdity of a man from the second eleven of an unknown club winning a test match. Sydney and Melbourne join London in 'appreciation of the greatest joke in the history of cricket'. And that is the end of Spedegue's career. His health has always been fragile, and his doctor declares that his heart would not stand any more.

Although a fanciful story, a mere bagatelle, it has a serious point, namely the limitations of orthodoxy. At a time when cricket and coaching methods were becoming standardised, the selectors' search for 'something new' is a comic rebuke to the conformity that Conan Doyle believed was inhibiting the game. Australia's star batter finds a way to deal with Spedegue's unique style of bowling, but his teammates discover that everything they've been taught is useless: 'The slogging bumpkin from the village green would have made a better job of Spedegue than did these great cricketers, to whom the orthodox method was the only way'.

The model for Doyle's fascination with experiment and novelty was Bernard Bosanquet, the man who invented the googly. In Bosanquet's first Test match appearance in England, the opening Test of the 1905 Ashes series, he took 8 for 107 in Australia's second innings and won the match for his country. This was one of only seven Tests he played, several more than Spedegue but characteristic of the short-lived careers of several subsequent mystery bowlers. Jack Iverson, the Australian spinner with a bent-finger grip, is the obvious example. He played in all five Tests of the

1950–1951 Ashes series in Australia, taking 21 wickets at 15.73, including 6/27 in the second innings of the third. Called up for this series at the age of 35, Iverson never played international or first-class cricket again. His seven innings during the series produced three runs, leaving him with a Test batting average of 0.75. He later suffered from depression and, at the age of 58, shot himself. Like Bosanquet, he developed his idiosyncratic grip – using the thumb and middle finger, the thumb pointing the ball in the direction it would break and enabling him to bowl leg-breaks, off-breaks and top-spinners without any change of action – from experimenting with a table-tennis ball. A later Australian spin bowler, Jack Gleeson, puzzled batters for several seasons in the late 1960s and early 1970s using Iverson's action.

'The Story of Spedegue's Dropper' also highlights the ubiquity of the lob, or donkey drop, in cricket stories of the early twentieth century as a style of bowling to be taken seriously. Spedegue is not just another example of a bowler with a comic action. In fact, his action is never described. Instead, it is the means by which he secures his dismissals that provides the comedy. The joke is on the batters, not the bowlers, as they struggle to deal with a delivery the likes of which they've never seen and find comic ways of getting out.

There's almost nothing comic, strange or implausible in cricket that hasn't happened before. In an article titled 'Some Recollections of Cricket' (1909), Doyle described the most humiliating dismissal he'd ever suffered. The bowler 'propelled (the ball) like a quoit into the air to a height of at least 30 feet, and it fell straight and true on to the top of the bails [...] To play it one would have needed to turn the blade of the bat straight up, and could hardly have failed to give a chance. I tried to cut it off my stumps, with the result that I knocked down my wicket and broke my bat, while the ball fell in the midst of this general chaos'.

Which brings me back to my opening. In the same article, Doyle describes a curious incident when facing a fast bowler named Bradley, one of the quickest in England at the time, while playing for the MCC against Kent.

His first delivery I hardly saw, and it landed with a terrific thud upon my thigh. A little occasional pain is one of the chances of cricket, and one takes it as cheerfully as one can, but on this occasion it suddenly became sharp to an unbearable degree. I clapped my hand to the spot, and found to my amazement that I was on fire. The ball had landed straight on a small tin vesta box in my trouser pocket, had splintered the box, and set the matches ablaze. It did not take me long to turn out my pocket and scatter the burning vestas over the grass [...] W.G. was greatly amused. 'Couldn't get you out – had to set you on fire!' he cried, in the high voice which seemed so queer from so big a body.

The novel that has more references to cricket and cricketers than any other is also the least read classic in the English literary canon, James Joyce's *Finnegans Wake* (1939). Joyce's brother, Stanislaus, described Joyce's 'eager interest in the game':

> I remember having to bowl for him for perhaps an hour in our back garden in Richmond Street. I did so out of pure goodness of heart since, for my part, I loathed the silly tedious, tedious, inconclusive game, and would not walk across the road to see a match.

Ranjitsinhji, Fry, Trumper and Spofforth were Joyce's particular heroes.

The sounds of cricket echo in one of the early episodes of *A Portrait of the Artist as a Young Man* (1916). Stephen Dedalus, a new boy at Clongowes Wood College, listens to some of his fellow pupils discussing how a group of older boys have been caught in the act of something wicked. No one seems sure of what it was. Someone suggests it was taking cash from the rector's study, another that it was quaffing the altar wine. As Stephen tries to catch what they're saying, he hears the sound of cricket from all over the playground. Boys are 'bowling twisters and lobs'; the bats are saying 'pick, pack, pock, puck'. Then comes the revelation: they were caught 'smugging', school slang for homosexual activity. The boys fall silent, and Stephen is bewildered. The sound of cricket bats slows: 'pick, pock'. Momentarily, we're back in the world of the public school cricket story and the relation of the sport to sex and flogging.

The Lotus-Eaters episode of *Ulysses* (1922) picks up this theme at a later time and in a different character, Leopold Bloom, as he makes his way through the streets of Dublin. Thoughts of his sexless marriage and his wife, Molly's, infidelity are forgotten as he visits the chemist, purchases a cake of soap and sets off for the Turkish baths with masturbation on his mind, anticipating the pleasure of 'Do(ing) it in the bath'. He pauses at the gates of Trinity College Park. 'Cricket weather', he thinks: 'Sit around under sunshades. Over after over. Out', before making his way to the Baths, anticipating 'his pale body reclined [...] at full, naked in a womb of warmth, oiled by scented melting soap, softly laved'.

It's a far cry from the sexual innocence and timidity of the schoolboy Stephen Dedalus, and the masturbatory fantasies of the 38-year-old advertising canvasser, Leopold Bloom – both episodes implicitly associated with cricket – to Joyce's account of the love-making of HCE (Humphrey Chimpden Earwicker) and ALP (Anna Livia Plurabelle) in *Finnegans Wake*. Anthony Burgess's description of Joyce's last novel as 'one of the few books of the world that can make us laugh aloud on nearly every page' is unlikely to be shared by most readers who've tackled it, but is certainly true of the two pages describing HCE and ALP having sex in a bedroom above a pub, a scene described entirely in terms of cricket and for my money the great comic tour-de-force of cricket in fiction.

HCE is enjoying 'her old stick-in-the block' and the way 'he was slogging his paunch about, elbiduubled' (these passages are best read aloud):

> whenever she druv behind her stumps for a tyddlesly wink through his tunniclifft bagslops after the rising bounder's yorkers, as he studd and stoddard and trutted and trumpered [...] it tickled her innings

A few notes might help. J. T. (Johnny) Tyldesley was a prolific scorer for Lancashire and England; John Tunnicliffe was nicknamed 'Long John of Pudsey'; A. E. Stoddard was a sportsman of great stamina who in 1886 scored 485 for Hampstead against the Stoics after a night of cards and dancing; A. E. Trott is the only man to have hit a cricket ball over the pavilion at Lord's; Joyce's boyhood hero Victor Trumper needs no elaboration, and on it goes: 'lordherry' (Lord Harris), 'ringeysingey' (Ranjitsinhji and his famed leg-glance), even the empsyseas, they're all there.

And so it reaches a climax:

> The game old merrimynn, square to leg [...] with his hobbsy socks and his wisden's bosse [...] and his gentleman's grip and his playaboy's plunge and his flannelly feelyfooling, treading her hump and hambledown like a maiden well held, ovalled over [...] (how's that? Noball, he carries his bat!) nine hundred and dirty too not out

And somewhere in all this wordplay, punning, double and triple entendre and literary referencing (Kipling's 'flannelled fools at the wicket' in the lines above) is 'the tarrant's brand on his hottoweyt brow', Frank Tarrant was the only cricketer to have taken a hat-trick and carried his bat in the same match, for Middlesex against Gloucester in 1909. HCE follows Tarrant's example in managing something similar.

And there is impiety as well as scatology in the novel's many references to cricket (said to number one hundred and sixty-eight). There are repeated allusions to Thomas Lord – 'the Lord's own day', 'the old Lord' and so on – and, of course, the cricketer who is named most often – Grace, 'a man of centuries', who figures as a version of HCE, fellow bearer of a paunch. From sweaty sex to our heavenly father, cricket serves for anything you can name.

By way of résumé, and for a last word on cricket and comedy, I turn to the second of Geoffrey Willans's and Ronald Searle's Molesworth books, *How to be Topp* (1954). Willans's sequence of drawings illustrating 'Batsmanship' begins with the batter's stance, the left leg raised, the toe pointing upwards. Unlike Grace and Reginald, however, not even his heel remains on the ground. The delivery he faces is conspicuously a lob. The batter's eye is raised skywards, and his swing of the bat looks like someone trying to swat a wasp. The ball comes down on his head, and his extravagant follow-through results in him demolishing the wickets and, like Conan Doyle, breaking his bat.

'Criket', according to Molesworth's headmaster, is all about 'the STRATE BAT. Keep yore bat strate boy and all will be all right in life as in criket'. Molesworth, however, finds it extremely difficult to play with a 'strate' bat and when he does he gets bowled anyway. He describes taking strike in terms that recall the blacksmith's opening delivery in Macdonell's *England, Their England*.

> Fast blower retreat with the ball mutering and cursing. He stamp on the grass with his grate hary feet he beat his chest and give grate cry. Then with a trumpet of rage he charge towards you. Quake quake ground tremble birdseed fly in all directions if only you can run away but it is not done. Grit teeth close eyes. Ball hit your pads and everyone go mad.
> OWSATSIR OW WASIT EHOUT!

And his 'soliloquy' while idly standing at 'mid-of' is a mock-epitaph of the public school cricket story, Eton as St Custard's.

Ah-me. As i stand here [...] how petty it all seme. These flaneled fules, the umpires, the headmaster who bask in his deck chair. All those latin books inside, the shavings in the carpentry shop the japes and wheezes – so much toil so much effort. And it may all be ended in a moment.

The accompanying drawing shows Molesworth, hands in pockets, unaware that he's about to be sconced by a descending ball.

His only consolation is that he'll be able to give it up when he grows up:

Then you rustle the paper and sa Wot a shocking show by m.c.c. most deplorable a lot of rabits ect. ect. Well, you kno how they go on. Enuff.

Chapter 5

CRICKET AND TRAGEDY

Strength, talent gone – then what to do?
Great Albert Trott, like Relf, was gunned down too
By his own hand in Willesden – very sad but true
— *Gavin Ewart, 'The Sadness of Cricket'*

For a game that has produced such a large number of suicides, there's surprisingly little tragic cricket fiction. War, yes, but the tragic war deaths in the public school stories I've discussed are only indirectly connected with cricket, and the cricket murder novel is primarily a form of entertainment. Bruce Hamilton's *Pro: An English Tragedy* (1946) stands out not only as a tragedy but also as one of the very few novels about county cricket and the professional game.

Bruce Hamilton, godson of Conan Doyle, was the older brother of Patrick Hamilton, author of the play *Gas Light* (1938), which became a celebrated 1944 film noir, and the critically admired 1940 novel *Hangover Square*. The brothers, whose father was an alcoholic and whose mother committed suicide, were both socialists with a fondness for cricket nurtured at the Sussex county ground at Hove. Bruce completed writing *Pro* in 1942 while living and teaching in Barbados, but its publication was delayed until after the Second World War.

Pro tells the story of a father and son – Albert and Teddy Lamb – professional cricketers with the fictional county team of Midhampton. Albert's career stretched from the beginning of the 1890s into the early years of the twentieth century, Teddy's either side of the First World War. Both were medium-fast bowlers and useful batters, county cricketers 'of the very first rank' but never quite of consistent test match quality. Albert, the son of a gamekeeper, had served a four-year apprenticeship on the Lord's ground staff, after which he returned to Midhampton and helped the newly founded minor county team to achieve county championship status, becoming the mainstay of its bowling attack.

Albert had hoped that his son's cricket career would follow a different course: Midhampton Grammar, a scholarship to Oxford or Cambridge, and a comfortable first-class career as an amateur. He saw that cricket was becoming commercialised and ruthless and had social aspirations for Teddy, understanding that 'a professional cricketer is by definition no gentleman'. But he loses all the money from his benefit match speculating in a failing mining venture, and then, on the last day of the county season, exhausted by the endless overs he's bowled throughout many summers, and by the physical wear and tear of his long career, he collapses on the field and dies.

There's no money left, and Teddy has to leave school and take up farm labouring. Several years later, now physically stronger, he is taken on to the Midhampton ground staff and begins the hard slog of a hopeful young pro. Hamilton's novel is all about the gritty realities and precarious financial existence of the life of a pro. Teddy's duties as a ground staff 'boy' involve mowing and rolling the wickets, marking out pitches, cleaning the pads and boots of the members and senior cricketers, oiling bats and binding the split ones. When he gets to touch a cricket ball it's often just to bowl to senior players who dislike having their wickets demolished. Occasionally several of the better players put coins on their stumps and, if they're lucky, the 'boys' might get a tip at the end of the session, but Midhampton's amateurs are less generous than Raffles. There's also the problem of the off-season when the meagre wages of the ground staff dry up. Teddy finds a job delivering medicines on his bike for a local doctor for dismally low pay.

When he is finally selected for his first county match, he is replaced on the morning of the game by a young public schoolboy, a gentleman recently arrived at the club. His eventual debut, against Sussex at Hove, is neither a triumph nor a disaster. There are no fairy tales in this novel. He bowls steadily, taking three wickets in the first innings and one in the second (the novel includes a scorecard), and he's retained for the final two games of the season. His following season is much more successful. He plays every match, takes the second-most wickets in the team and inches his way up the batting order from the bottom to number nine.

But then comes war. One sunny afternoon in late August, Midhampton, playing at home, is chasing down a stiff total:

Just after four o'clock a sound of brassy music was heard, and presently a company of khaki-clad soldiers headed by a regimental band, appeared in the ground. Passing through a gap at the south end, where the heavy roller stood, the soldiers unexpectedly marched right on to the playing pitch, paying no attention to the cricketers, who had to move out of the way. Orders were barked, platoons formed, drill manoeuvres executed. The players watched the performances for a few minutes, looking rather sheepish. Then as the umpires pulled up the stumps, they trooped off. It was the last of county cricket in Midhampton for nearly five years.

It's a remarkable scene, an abruptly dramatic way of rendering how the First World War brought cricket to a halt.

When cricket resumes after the war, there is an acute shortage of players. Some of the Midhampton players have been killed, some wounded too badly to continue playing, others grown too old to continue their careers. Teddy, who has suffered nothing worse than a wounded foot, finds himself one of the few experienced players left.

The character of the game is changing too, along the lines Teddy's father had anticipated. Jim Revill, Midhampton's star batter, though a professional, has the manner and style of an amateur. He dresses immaculately and seems to have money to burn. When Teddy asks him where 'all the dough comes from', Revill shows him a full-page advert for 'Kleenodent' featuring his radiant toothy smile. Other product endorsements include 'Luster for the hair', the 'Jim Revill bat' with a royalty on every one sold and a ghosted column in a national newspaper. As Dorothy Sayers had written, 'it pays to advertise'. Even more traditional forms of earning for the pro, like the coaching at minor public schools that helped sustain Joseph Wells, have been upgraded – 'not the usual round, you know, but Dukes and Jews and Rajahs and big pots generally who want to get their boys into the Eton eleven', Revill tells Teddy.

A new kind of pro is emerging even among those who lack the glamour and earning capacity of Revill, 'new young men [...] with no very noticeable reverence for their superiors'. Their envy of the generous expense accounts quietly enjoyed by many amateurs on the country circuit differs from the grudging class-based attitudes towards gentlemen cricketers of Albert and Teddy's time. This new breed of pro is not opposed to social privilege but wishes to be part of it. And they are hostile to socialism. When cricket is suspended during the 1926 General Strike, they join up with the Organisation for the Maintenance of Supplies, headed by Midhampton's amateur captain, Oxford Blue and ex-Army officer Nigel Le Mesurier, who describes the strike as 'war'. Only Teddy and several of his pre-war teammates resist the call to arms.

Teddy's career flourishes in the mid-1920s when, to overcome the dead pitches that groundsmen of the time were preparing, he develops a form of leg theory, directing his inswingers and off-cutters at the leg stump to a packed leg-side field. This technique, a prototype of bodyline but without the barrage of short-pitched deliveries, brings instant success, short-lived fame and selection for an MCC tour of the West Indies. It's at this point that the shadow of tragedy, which has hovered around Teddy's story from the beginning, starts to take definite shape.

Early in the tour, while batting against Barbados, he is knocked out by a fast, short-pitched delivery. Unconscious for several days, he is shipped home, loses out on the payments the tour would have brought him and misses the first half of the next home season because of persistent head-aches from his concussion. When he is able to play again, Le Mesurier puts a stop to his leg theory, declaring it unsporting. His figures and his earnings suffer, and the already tense relations with his captain become bitter. He's tempted by an offer to play Lancashire League cricket which Hamilton characteristically spells out in full detail: a five-year contract at £350 per year for four months of cricket, plus talent money, collections taken on the ground for particularly good performances and potential earnings from private coaching. But the League is frowned on by the MCC and the county authorities who regard the commercialisation it has brought to the game as contrary to the spirit of cricket. His socially aspiring wife can't bear Lancashire people, and so he turns down an offer which would have ensured some financial security when his career comes to an end.

Frustrated by Le Mesurier's ban on leg theory, he turns to leg-spin, reckoning that slow bowlers don't have 'their bodies worn out by hours of plugging away on lifeless pitches'. He develops a serviceable googly and enjoys reasonable success until his shoulder packs up. 'Googlyitis' is the diagnosis – 'hardly a muscle or a tendon in your right shoulder that hasn't been torn or displaced', the doctor tells him – and his bowling career comes to an end. How the livelihood of a pro depended on avoiding injury. Over the years, he's become a useful batter and he now develops this side of his game with some success. But he's earning less and is paying a third of his reduced income to his ex-wife in alimony. His upcoming benefit match is crucial to his future.

The success or failure of a testimonial match depended on the weather. The beneficiary was responsible for the match wages of the players, umpires and ground staff, and his actual benefit only amounted to what was left from the gate takings and collections taken each day at the ground. Bad weather could be insured against, but the premium was high. Teddy opted for limited rather than full cover and was relieved when the first day shone bright. A heart-warming ovation from the crowd, his quickfire innings of 77 and a promising forecast made for a rewarding day. Overnight, however, a thunderstorm broke and the second day was washed out. The final day's weather was perfect, but the pitch had been ruined, the opposition, Northants, was skittled out twice, and the match finished early. Teddy helped to spoil his own party by taking five slip catches. After paying off the insurance premium, he benefited to the sum of seventeen pounds.

His life is now one of slow decline and fall. His troubles are partly the result of poor choices and bad luck, but fundamentally a consequence of life as a county pro. Teddy's body starts to let him down. An attack of lumbago, the result of many years of 'the eternal up and down' of fielding in the slips, sees him move to mid-on where his lack of mobility is exposed. His timing begins to fall away as he sees the ball less quickly and hurries his strokes. Towards the end of the season following his benefit, he's told that his contract won't be renewed. His final match is at the same venue as his first, against Sussex at Hove. The pro's life has come full circle. The crowd gives him a warm reception, Duleepsinhji comes and pats him on the back and the Sussex bowlers offer him a few soft deliveries. The moment is touching but carries no future.

Thrown onto the labour market in early middle age with no qualifications except his knowledge of cricket, Teddy's only course is umpiring. But first, there's the winter to get through. He has just fifty pounds in savings and is forced to leave his lodgings and find board in the poorest quarter of the town, 'a slum, airless, insanitary, decaying'. He's appointed to the list of second-class umpires, and for the next two years serves a new kind of apprenticeship as he waits for promotion to the first-class list. This brings some relief, but the work is exhausting and demeaning:

six hours' work, six days a week, work that would keep him on his feet the whole time, and demanding unremitting vigilance and concentration. A superficial respect for his office would be observed but not for his person [...] His mistakes would be noted, players discontented with his decisions would, behind his back, accuse him of ignorance, prejudice, partisanship, and even corruption.

Hamilton's view of the pro world of this time admits no illusions. The crucial thing, as ever, is money. As a first-class umpire, Teddy reckons that he can save forty or fifty pounds each year so that in 15 or 20 years' time when he retires, he should have put aside around a thousand pounds. But his back continues to trouble him, and his concentration is affected. Several times he makes mistakes in calling the over, his attention is caught wandering at square leg when there's an appeal for a stumping, and he falls foul of his nemesis, Le Mesurier, when he rules that a catch his former captain claims to have taken was scooped off the ground. At the county captains' end-of-season meeting, Teddy's name is removed from both the first-class and minor counties list of umpires.

The only work he can now find is in a local pub, and his drinking, an off-and-on problem in recent years, becomes heavier. His lumbago is chronic, and the headaches he suffered after his concussion in Barbados return and intensify. He loses his job and is reduced to delivering newspapers, a boy's job with a boy's wage. The bottom rung of the ladder he's been slipping down is reached when, out of pity he's given a job selling scorecards at his old county ground. Ill and drinking ever more heavily, he causes a disruption at an August Bank Holiday match and is barred from the ground. Publicly shamed and with all dignity lost, Teddy returns to his squalid room, digs out his scrapbooks of press cuttings recording 'the dash he had once cut in the world' – his *Wisdens,* even the one in which he'd figured as a Cricketer of the Year, have been sold for beer – and slowly, lovingly turns the pages. Shutting the last of the books, he gathers up his few remaining coppers, puts a penny in the metre, opens the oven door and lights the flame.

Prolepsis, the rhetorical figure of anticipation, is a recurring feature of *Pro,* helping to underline its tragic character. The theme of suicide has first been made explicit when Teddy returns from the war and, amid the other fatalities, learns of the suicide of a former Midhampton slow bowler, Chris Burton, who, reduced to extreme poverty after retirement, had cut his throat. Teddy is disturbed but takes comfort from the benefit he knows will eventually come his way and from the coaching engagements he has begun to pick up. The warning of Burton's end is quickly forgotten.

Suicide has been hinted at from the very beginning of Teddy's county career. On his debut at Hove he is dismissed by Relf (A. E.), the initials coming after the surname indicating a professional. This is Albert Relf, a real-life county pro and stalwart of Sussex for more than twenty years, during which time he made over 22,000 runs, took almost 1,900 wickets and played 13 test matches for England. He was named one of *Wisden's* Five Cricketers of the Year at the age of 39 and continued playing county cricket until he was 47. On retiring, he became cricket coach at Wellington College in Berkshire where, in 1937, in a state of depression, he shot himself through the heart in the College's cricket pavilion.

Relf, a medium-pace bowler renowned for his ability to sustain long spells – he once bowled unchanged against Essex for seven hours – is a kind of model for Teddy, whose bowling is similar in style and stamina to Relf's. Bruce Hamilton and his brother Patrick would have spent many hours at Hove when they were young, admiring the physical endurance of this county workhorse.

Hamilton, like many cricket fiction writers, liked to mix the names of the real with the fictive, as we see when Duleepsinhji pats Teddy on the back as he walks out for his last innings at Hove. Sussex cricketers, as David Frith observed in *Silence of the Heart: Cricket Suicides* (2001), have figured heavily among those many cricketers who have taken their own lives. Hamilton's inclusion of Relf in a novel written soon after the suicide of this hard-working Sussex bowler is doing particular work as a foreshadowing of Teddy's tragic fate, and is also more broadly typical of the life of many professional cricketers at that time.

Pro was very much in Anthony Quinn's mind when writing *Half of the Human Race* (2011). Set back in the 'Golden Age' of cricket, the years either side of the First World War, the main focus of its cricket narrative is A. E. Tamburlaine – 'The Great Tam' – a famous Test cricketer whose career is fading. In the character of Tam, Quinn wrote, he 'wanted to express the poignancy of the great sportsman facing the end of a career which […] feels like the end of a life […] a painful slide into oblivion'.

We first see Tam through the eyes of Connie Callaway, a young suffragette and cricket lover, at the Priory in Brighton, M-shire's county ground: 'a tall, broad-shouldered figure with a heavy moustache and a striped club tie raffishly belted around his waist'. She checks out his *Wisden* profile: 'debut for Sussex, 1889 [...] one of the Five Cricketers of the Year in 1893; 16 Test appearances [...] *annus mirabilis* in 1899, when he hit four centuries in successive matches and scored the quickest hundred (44 minutes) in county history; moved to M-shire, 1906'. But he's most famous for having hit the ball over the Lord's pavilion when playing for the MCC against Sussex in 1905. 'Only been done once before', Will Maitland, a rising star of the county circuit and foil to the older cricketer, tells Connie as he shows her his proudest possession, the bat Tam had used on that occasion, 'running his palm along the varnished blade in reverent absorption'. Tam's bat figures as a kind of sacred relic in the novel.

Tam had turned pro at 18, and his glittering career has left him much more financially secure than a journeyman cricketer like Teddy Lamb. It's the psychological impact of his declining powers rather than the lack of money that haunts the closing years of his cricket career. Early in the novel, even before his batting has begun to decline, he remarks to Will: 'This game [...] it preys on doubt'. Why, he wonders, is it that some days you can middle every ball and other days not at all. But, he concludes with a shrug, that's just cricket. Eventually, however, his reflexes begin to slow, his stats dip, a long innings leaves his knee feeling as if it's on fire, his mother is dying and his captain notices alcohol on his breath when he turns up to nets in the morning. He's now 44, his career is in its twilight, but he's reluctant to admit this until finally, on the point of being sacked, he walks.

Several months later, Tam has lunch with Connie in London. Connie, grateful for the support Tam has given her while she's in Holloway prison for hurling a brick through the window of a government minister as part of the suffragette campaign (described as like throwing in to the keeper from the outfield), has bought him *The Poems of Francis Thompson*. She draws his attention to 'At Lord's', which is also Quinn's epigraph to the novel:

'For the field is full of shades as I near the shadowy coast,
And a ghostly batsman plays to the bowling of a ghost,
And I look through my tears on a soundless-clapping host
As the run-stealers flicker to and fro,
To and fro: -
O my Hornby and my Barlow long ago!

How cricket is haunted by its past.

Tam talks to Connie about his loss of a future. Umpiring doesn't appeal, he jokes grimly. Nor do the Lancashire leagues which have been making offers. The trouble with cricket, he says, is that when you reach the top too young it's 'a long slide down', a line taken from the 1953 film *The Final Test*, its script by the playwright Terence Rattigan. He muses on how difficult it is to leave the game behind and tells Connie the story of a Sussex batter he used to open with. This man, Usher, was regularly barracked by the home crowd for his painfully slow scoring, but after he retired, was unable to live without the game and shot himself in his lodgings in Eastbourne.

Quinn acknowledges his debt to David Frith's *Silence of the Heart,* and Usher is clearly based on William Scotton, who played for Nottinghamshire and England in the 1880s and whose sad story Frith recounts. Scotton, like Usher, was a pathological worrier and stone-waller, the subject not only of crowd derision but also of a parody tribute in *Punch*.

'Block, block, block, at the foot of thy wicket, O Scotton!
And I would that my tongue could utter my boredom.'

The parody is of Tennyson's 'Break, break, break, / On thy cold gray stones, O Sea! / And I would that my tongue could utter / The thoughts that arise in me'. Sacked by Nottinghamshire in 1891, divorced and further depressed by the pressures of umpiring which he'd taken up, he slit his throat in his lodgings.

By this point, the ominous associations of Tam's initials 'A. E.' are becoming apparent. A. E. Trott, the other cricketer referred to by Will as having hit the ball over Lord's pavilion, shot himself through the head in his lodgings on the eve of the First World War. And A. E. Stoddard, whom Joyce singled out as the exemplar of athletic stamina, was the other most famous example of cricketing suicide from this time, a man who captained England at rugby as well as cricket and was renowned for his late-night exploits. Tam, we learn, had lived a similar sort of life as a young cricketer. By the late 1890s, however, Stoddard's stellar reputation had been tarnished by press stories that he'd compromised his amateur status by taking money beyond the expenses he was entitled to. His mother died, so often it seems a trigger for cricketers of the period to fall into depression, and his knee began to seriously trouble him. Retiring, he turned to golf and whisky, money worries accumulated and his marriage soured. On Easter Sunday 1915, he retired to bed and shot himself. It's a grim irony that when captain of England, Stoddard had made the first declaration in Test history.

There are recurring, almost standard, features in these and other cases of cricketing suicide: Money, injury, a mother's death, the end of a career leaving the cricketer with a profound sense of loss that develops into alcoholism and depression. Tam's lunch with Connie takes us further inside these familiar symptoms, to cricket being 'so much about nerves' and yet the hollowness of a life without it: 'At least when you're on your own in the field you know you're there for a purpose', he tells Connie. During their lunch, Tam is accosted by a fashionably dressed young man 'with a monocle gleaming in his eye and a grin as toothy as an alligator's', one of the so-called 'nuts' also described in *Pro* – 'pale young exquisites [...] with vacuous oval faces and names like Algy or Reggie or Archie' – who remembers Tam's famous shot at Lord's. Nothing could be more painful than the idolatry of a 'jackass', as Tam describes him, and to be reminded of the highlight of a life he's lost and which seems to have become its only point.

By now, there's a near-epidemic of suicides in Quinn's novel. Connie has recently learnt that her father's death some years earlier was a suicide, and we're reminded that Tam's father, a travelling salesman who'd fallen into debt and turned to drink, had hung himself. And so, a few weeks later, the inevitable. During Festival Week at the Priory, and on the eve of his testimonial match, which will also be his farewell appearance – that moment described by the Australian cricketer and writer Jack Fingleton as when a cricketer 'is no more, nor ever will be again' – Tam is found dead in his lodgings, having shot himself through the temple.

Quinn's Tam is an amalgam of Stoddart and Trott, with Teddy Lamb also there in the mix. *Half of the Human Race* is a kind of homage to both Hamilton and Frith's work, even down to Quinn's use of names from *Pro* – Revill, for example, a member of both Teddy and Tam's teams. Most of all, there is the curious case of the recurring initials A. E. - Relf, Stoddart, Trott and Tam. Their famous contemporary, the poet A. E. Housman, author of *A Shropshire Lad*, should count himself lucky to have died peacefully at home at the age of 77.

Tragedy needs a setting, and Hamilton and Quinn find this in the structure, organisation and practices of cricket in the years between the founding of the county championship in 1890 and the end of the Second World War. There's nothing in Teddy's nature that makes him particularly vulnerable to the risk of suicide. It is the pressures of the professional game of the period, the inequalities and exploitation of its class structure and the financial insecurity this brings, its lack of reward for the labour expended by the pro and the toll it takes on his body, all of which leave him without a future when he is sacked or retires. Hamilton's great achievement is to capture the life of a pro so convincingly and in such detail, and to show how the tragedy of Teddy's end, in the ironically understated remark of the county secretary, Mr Gaul, is not 'entirely his own fault'.

The life of a pro changed out of recognition in the decades after the Second World War, and some of the potential for treating the professional life of a cricketer as a subject for tragedy disappeared as a result. Yet, suicide among cricketers has persisted, most recently the tragic case of Graham Thorpe, and so too has the question as to whether there's something inherent in the game itself that is responsible.

The story of Peter Roebuck is another tragic contemporary example of cricketing suicide. A regular county cricketer for Somerset by the age of 18, his career could be seen as an illustration of Tam's plaint about the dangers of reaching the top too young. Although Roebuck never quite reached the top, he had a long and successful county career, was a Wisden Cricketer of the Year in 1988 and found a busy life after retirement as a cricket writer and broadcaster. In Cape Town in 2011, after being questioned by the police about an alleged sexual assault, he jumped to his death from the sixth floor of his hotel. Sex rather than alcohol appears to have been the trigger – every such story has its own specificities – but otherwise Roebuck's story follows the general pattern of many of Frith's examples.

Two years before his death, Roebuck wrote a piece for *Cricinfo*, 'Johnson, Hughes and the ordeal of cricket', about the trials those two Australian cricketers were experiencing in that year's Ashes series. In the course of this, there's a succinctly telling description of the stresses of cricket: 'Cricket is an isolating and yet public game. Soccer players suffer when they miss a penalty. Cricketers risk that collapse every time they go out to bat. It is not a sport at all. It's an execution.' Mike Brearley makes a similar point in his introduction to Frith's book but draws a different conclusion from it. For Roebuck, the batter is living on the edge with every ball, under the blade or with the noose around their neck. Brearley, on the other hand, sees this state of constant jeopardy as helping the batter to anticipate the experience of loss that retirement brings by forcing them to come to terms with symbolic death each time they're dismissed and return to the pavilion. Who is right? Is going out to bat like facing death, or is dismissal a learning experience that should help the cricketer come to terms with the loss of their profession upon retirement? Either way, cricket, life and death are interwoven in a manner that few, if any, other sports are. Father Time, the Lord's weather vane, hangs forebodingly over all cricketing careers. It's surprising there aren't more examples of cricket fiction that explore this.

J. L. Carr's *A Season in Sinji* (1967) uses an entirely different setting – that of war and empire – for its tragedy, turning its back on the traditional English locations of cricket fiction and looking ahead to the post-colonial cricket novel I'll discuss in the following chapter.

Carr was worried that Alan Ross, who published his novel, might be put off by the cricket. Ross, who had played county cricket for Northamptonshire and was the *Observer* cricket correspondent, also a poet and sometime editor of the literary journal *London Magazine*, was quick to reassure him: 'I don't know why you think the cricket might put me off [...] The cricket put me ON'.

Carr himself was no mean cricketer, perhaps the most proficient of any of the novelists discussed in this book. Ted Dexter is the obvious exception, but his writing disqualifies him. Byron Rogers, Carr's biographer, describes him as a batter of near Minor Counties standard. He scored his last century at the age of 57 and continued playing for a decade after that. Best known for his Booker short-listed and Guardian Fiction prize-winning novel *A Month in the Country* (1980), among cricket cognoscenti he is also famous for his *Dictionary of Extra-Ordinary Cricketers* (1983), one of many small format books he published through his own Quince Tree Press. This one sold 10,000 copies within a month of its publication. He also produced the annual Northamptonshire County Cricket League Handbook, a fixture list with player averages, another little book designed for the pocket. His last published work was a book review in the 1993 *Wisden*.

In fact, although Carr initially titled his novel *A Game of Cricket*, cricket matches as such are a small part of it. *A Season in Sinji* is nevertheless suffused with the game. At the very beginning, the narrator, Flanders, reflects how the 'whole business [of his story] was like a game of cricket, the issue never sure, who'd win, who'd lose'. The business of his novel includes almost everything – war, death, empire, love, sex, comedy, tragedy, absurdity, futility – and cricket is used throughout to capture and figure these large themes as well as many smaller passing moments.

Flanders's story opens at the beginning of the Second World War with him in an RAF training camp, waiting to be posted overseas. There he meets Wakerley, who becomes his particular friend, and Turton, an over-bearing and vindictive leading aircraftsman who will become the *bete noir* of both men. The three of them are posted together to RAF Bathurst in the Gambia, on the coast of West Africa, where Turton persecutes them both and obstructs Flanders's plan to put together a cricket team of non-commissioned officers to challenge the officer teams in the RAF colony.

The novel makes pervasive use of cricket references and figures of speech. Flanders's mother oils his cricket bats in the loft while he's away at war, a distinctive form of keeping the home fires burning. The compli-cations of Flanders's duties as a photographer on Catalina flying boats, tracking and recording enemy vessels and processing the photos in the darkroom, are compared to 'opening an innings on that kind of heavy afternoon when the new ball swings like a boomerang'. The most bizarre comparison with cricket is during the novel's concluding scene in which Flanders and Turton are marooned in a dinghy after their flying boat has been shot down over the Atlantic. Flanders describes the appalling heat: 'You couldn't get away from it. It was like a crazy rule of the I Zingari Club, I remember reading – "New members will take their stand in the nets without bat or pads for a period to be decided upon by a commit-tee member present and there remain whilst being bowled at by other members"'.

The cricket match itself, which provided the novel's original title, is less than five pages long, though the build-up stretches over many more. Flanders, a highly competent batter, conceives a plan to put together an irregular team from his own small squadron after watching a couple of officer teams in a league run by the Station Sports Committee 'scratching about like old hens on a midden'. He gathers together a ragbag team – 'three real cricketers and eight makeweights' – and sets up an alternative league in which the officer teams condescendingly agree to participate. Despite the refusal of Station Headquarters to lend them any kit for prac-tice, Flanders's irregulars start to defeat the officer teams and eventually make it to the final. At this point, the Station Sports Committee steps in. Flanders is demoted, Turton is made captain and several of Flanders's bet-ter regular players are replaced by incompetent officers.

Turton wins the toss and puts the Station XI in. Matches were played on the parade ground: 'There wasn't a blade of grass on it and, once past a fielder, every shot was a certain boundary – the ball ran like a hare on the baked earth.' Turton, who provides another example of a droll bowling action – fancy, overlong run-up, 'windmilling arms [...] both feet pedalling the air which [...] ballsed up his rhythm' – over-bowls himself. Flanders is banished to the outfield, what's left of the regular team loses heart and at half-past five the Station side declares at 217 for 3.

In reply, the officer ring-ins open for the irregulars and are quickly dismissed. Flanders comes to the wicket with the score at 3 for 5. Batting at the other end is Wood, a backstreet London kid who looks as though he'd 'learnt to play with a home-made bat and a cork ball in a council school playground'. He has no strokes at all but is very determined. Dropping his bat 'like a hen-house shutter', his hands bleeding after a barrage of deliveries from the Station fast bowler, he sticks it out. At the other end, Flanders lets anything wide of his off stump go through to the keeper, except when taking a single at the end of the over to protect Wood. Between them, they grind out eight runs in the 10 overs.

Turton has been shouting at Flanders from the boundary to get a move on, and when he comes in to bat after Wood is dismissed, he commands Flanders to take some quick singles. Flanders refuses his first call, and Turton is run-out, stranded at Flanders's end, yelling at him 'like a maniac'. The next man follows Flanders's lead, 'sitting astride his bat' and smothering everything.

As the light fades, Turton comes onto the field and orders Flanders to retire. Flanders ignores him. He knows the rules: A captain can declare an innings but can't retire a single player against his will. It grows darker and darker, but Flanders refuses to appeal against the light. Finally, the umpires are forced to call it a day: '217 for 3 them, 27 for 5 us. A draw!'

Next morning, Flanders is summoned to a meeting of the Station Sports Council where Turton accuses Flanders of usurping his authority as captain and persuading the rest of his team to sabotage the game. The outraged council members go on and on 'about Sportsmanship, Cricket being more than a Game, how it had shaped our Nation, etcetera, etcetera [...]'. They declare Flanders an unsuitable person for cricket and ban him from ever playing again at the Station. The proceedings remind Flanders of 'those absurd meetings of holy prefects in boarding school stories'. Nevertheless, Flanders admits to himself, Turton had really won: 'He'd beaten me [...] I'd built up that team to win that last Game, not to stop the other side winning'. His plan has failed.

Cricket in *A Season in Sinji* stands for life in its entirety. Early in the novel, waiting in camp for his posting overseas, Flanders muses: 'Half the world's trouble [...] is because there's no plan and we lose half the Test Matches for the same reason [...]' Having a plan and seeing it out is the *raison d'etre* of the squadron team. Plans give meaning; without them what is there? But by the novel's close, Flanders, adrift in a dinghy off the coast of West Africa with the man who has destroyed his plan, concludes: 'Plan! There was no plan. You could organise the little things and kid yourself there was some system, but the big thing, Life itself, was a sprawling, shapeless, disgusting mess. It had about as much plan as a sow's litter.' This bleak vision on which the novel ends has shadowed Flanders's story throughout its African scenes. When Wakerley is tragically killed in a plane crash, Flanders reflects on how 'we all go noisily from silence to silence', a note of existential melancholy rarely heard in cricket fiction.

A Season in Sinji is transparently autobiographical. It includes a frontispiece photograph of Carr himself standing alone on the Station's bare, dusty cricket ground, and another, incorporated into the text itself, of Carr and his team, bare-chested and lined up for a game of cricket. Byron Rogers' description of Carr in the Gambia serves as an account of Flanders as well: 'A young and hitherto self-contained Yorkshireman, brought up a strict Methodist [...] trying to make sense of the huge insanity of service life'. Cricket and war are no strangers to each other in fiction, but in Carr's hands, the tragic heroism that featured so strongly in earlier treatments of this theme has vanished. Instead, there is futility and despair.

A decisive reason for this difference is the novel's context of empire. The Gambia, where Flanders is posted, had been a British colony from the late eighteenth century until gaining independence in 1965. Sierra Leone, to where Carr was transferred later in the war, was founded as a British colony in 1808 to resettle returning Africans after the abolition of the slave trade and remained under British control until independence in 1961.

Carr's Sinji is a composite of these two neighbouring colonies with the indigenous population a mere backdrop. Flanders admits to a colour prejudice he can't conquer, and his view of Africa and its people echoes the generalised colonial distaste of British soldiers and administrators for the populations they governed. Strolling with Wakerley towards 'a Wog village', he describes how 'Africa is full of things to stare at': 'Women with faces eaten half away, mouths gaping from temple to cheek, men with elephantiasis, their testicles hanging to their knees, or sometimes a leg or an arm as thick as a tree trunk'.

The only moment of interaction between the men of the station and the local inhabitants is a disturbing scene of casual colonial violence around the midpoint of the novel. Returning from a cricket match against the Navy, the one occasion when Flanders plays for The Station XI, the lorry in which they're travelling is forced to halt in a native village because of a mechanical problem. The lorry stops under a mango tree, the team becomes bored with the delay, and someone starts shying mangos at one of the village houses. Others, Turton among them, join in.

> Some hit corrugated roofs like drum beats, one hit an old man, a child began to scream as he was struck on the back of the head as he ran for shelter. It was all hell let loose. Those mango were heavier than apples – more like cricket balls, except they burst when they landed. The blacks must have thought us fiends.

Turton approaches several women carrying earthenware pitchers of water on their heads, takes up a broom and pretends to use it as a billiard cue to pot the pitcher off the head of one of them. Encouraged by the laughter of his teammates, he starts poking the jars, causing them to topple. One of the women catches her jar before it falls to the ground, but all the water spills. Another grabs at hers 'like a half-asleep fielder', drops it, and the pitcher smashes, leaving her howling and drenched. 'Half the chaps were hooting, and about half were pretending not to notice'.

Flanders' role in this is unclear, but we've earlier seen him deliberately push a little boy, who is offering his 12-year-old sister for sex, off his bike. Flanders is sexually uptight, and this scene might imply he is prompted by moral outrage. But the tone of both these passages is disturbing, and the comparison of the broken pitcher to a dropped catch makes cricket itself complicit. When Flanders dismisses Turton's violence as 'simply stupid', adding that 'black women were used to rough treatment from their menfolk', Wakerley is provoked into challenging him:

> Sometimes I think Turton and you are brothers under the skin – Fascists. And for Pete's sake stop calling these people 'blacks' – they have a country too. Call them Africans.

This outburst reverses the dominant point of view of these episodes but is a rare corrective moment in Flanders's narrative.

It also places *A Season in Sinji* in the wider context of other literary fiction of empire, E. M. Forster's *A Passage to India* (1924) for example. The naming of characters in Carr's fiction is often pointed, and Turton is an unmistakable echo of Mr Turton, the British colonial official, and his rabidly racist wife in Forster's novel. Even the titles of these two novels suggest each other. Carr himself had been travelling in Burma when the Second World War broke out, and Orwell's *Burmese Days* (1934) is another novel of empire with parallels in *A Season in Sinji*. Flory, the main protagonist of Orwell's novel, and Wakerley in Carr's, are both uneasily positioned within the power relations of empire, caught between two worlds. The marginality of both men is underlined by physical signs of their not quite fitting, a facial birthmark in Flory's case and a stutter in Wakerley's. Fielding, the British headmaster of the college for Indians in *A Passage to India* is another example of the recurring figure in the fiction of empire of the man who's not really 'one of us'.

But Joseph Conrad was the novelist of colonialism who most influenced *A Season in Sinji*. Carr received what he called his 'first stiff dose of Conrad' at secondary school, and two of Conrad's most famous shorter works, 'Heart of Darkness' (1899) and 'The Secret Sharer' (1909), are strong presences in Carr's novel (the latter also figures in his best-known work, *A Month in the Country*). Conrad's influence is particularly apparent in the concluding episode of *A Season in Sinji* in which Flanders and Turton, two men alone and adrift in a dinghy on the Atlantic, mirror the situation of Marlow and Kurtz in *Heart of Darkness*, another pair of secret sharers as they make their torrid journey in a creaking steamboat back down the Congo River towards the Atlantic coast. Turton sits facing Flanders, totally silent, his eyes open but sightless, his breathing like that of a man under water, his face expressionless. There's no shade and the heat is intense. Flanders reflects on how like a game of cricket the story of Turton and himself has been, and how the game, if you could still call it that, was now at its end.

> I lost something at Sinji, and its last shred went that afternoon. Those last hours with Turton destroyed what I thought I was. We all lost […] Me last of all – because until then, I still believed every game must have a winner.

On the point of death, Turton's hand slowly stretches out towards Flanders, 'inch by inch, till the fingers reached my wrist and fastened on to it', like a mute Ancient Mariner grabbing the wedding guest in Coleridge's poem. By dawn, Turton is dead. Flanders eases the body over the side and sits alone, 'shivering in the baffling heat [...] sobbing on and on until darkness fell, bringing the rain'. Kurtz and Turton both die, Marlow and Flanders survive but are left with only their bitter stories to tell.

What has this to do with cricket? *A Season in Sinji* folds cricket into a requiem for empire, the stalemate of its cricket match quashing Henry Newbolt's refrain. The idea of 'playing the game' has lost all meaning, and together with its bleak aftermath, the novel signals the end of an era. In earlier fiction of war, death and empire, cricket embodied the ethos of sportsmanship, patriotism and valiant sacrifice. As Rupert Brooke put it in his poem 'The Soldier': 'If I should die, think only this of me: / That there's some corner of a foreign field / That is for ever England'. For Brooke, the dust of the English dead will enrich the soil of lesser climes, a sort of posthumous colonisation. In a late colonial setting such as Carr's Sinji, however, cricket, rather than expressing the unity of a nation at war, becomes the setting for a passive mutiny of men against officers, an ugly and absurd house match on a foreign field. A game of cricket intended to give point and meaning to the degraded life in which Flanders is caught has proved futile and absurd.

As if to underline this, Flanders imagines the legacy of cricket the RAF station will leave behind derisively expressed in the voice of Wakerley: 'In 2000 A.D. anthropologists will f-find a new tribe with a Fertility Dance exactly twenty-two yards long. With a Freudian t-terminology – maidens, b-balls, no-balls and bum balls'. But in fact, the legacy of cricket and its fiction in the post-colonial and global world has proved very different from Flanders's narrative and prediction.

Chapter 6

POST-COLONIAL AND GLOBAL CRICKET FICTION

The Indian people had taken the English game and made it their own.

–Mike Marqusee, *Slow Turn*

Cricket is probably the most intricately catalogued subject on the worldwide web aside from porn.

–Shehan Karunatilika

The renowned Sri Lankan novelist Michael Ondaatje, author of *The English Patient*, praised Shehan Karunatilaka's novel *Chinaman* (2011) for the way in which it refreshed 'the great fictional possibilities of cricket'. In earlier chapters, I have been solely concerned with English cricket fiction, emphasising that for all its comedy, sentimentality and nostalgia it also engaged with momentous events: how public schoolboys exchanged their cricket bats for rifles in the First World War; the aftermath and social consequences of that war; shifting ideas of class, gender and sexuality as the twentieth century wore on; the tragedy inherent in the game. By the final quarter of the century, however, the traditional narratives and settings of cricket fiction were exhausted and the new directions the game was taking were ignored. Cricket fiction needed to expand its territory and explore new worlds, to address the hitherto unspoken issue of race, for example, and turn its gaze on cricket's relation to a post-colonial, multicultural and global world, in short, to create new stories.

The first novel to do this was Mike Marqusee's *Slow Turn* (1988). Mike Marqusee was a polymath: a journalist, political activist and prolific writer whose many books ranged from politics, popular culture, music (two books on Bob Dylan), art and literature to the Indian subcontinent, health and cricket. Born in New York in 1953, he came to England in 1971 where he lived until his untimely death from bone marrow cancer in 2015. A self-described 'deracinated New York Marxist Jew', he'd come to love cricket while studying at the University of Sussex and watching county matches, yet another writer to have been nurtured at Hove. He was himself a keen cricketer although, as his obituarist Colin Robinson wrote, to see him batting was to be persuaded of the truth of the adage that 'the pen was mightier than the sword'.

As a cricket writer, Marqusee is best known for two books, *Anyone but England: An Outsider Looks at English Cricket* (1994) and *War Minus the Shooting* (1997), about the 1996 Cricket World Cup. However, the first book he ever published was a cricket novel, *Slow Turn* (1988). Long out of print and now rarely mentioned in accounts of Marqusee's writing career, it is a groundbreaking work in the history of cricket and fiction, a novel that takes English cricket into the world of politics and sport, rebel tours, big money, venture capitalism and financial corruption.

Slow Turn opens with an eye-catching sentence: 'In Madras the umpire was murdered and it made us all uneasy'. The novel is, among many other things, another cricket murder mystery. The narrator and main protagonist, Dave Stott, is part of an English touring side playing a series of exhibition matches sponsored by the Commercial Trust Bank of Southern India. The team, as Stott describes it, is 'a motley crew' made up of rising stars, ex-Test players and 'old county pros'. Stott is one of the latter, a left-handed batter whose early promise has faded and has recently, at the age of 30 and after 10 years of repetitive county slog, been let go by his county. He's surprised but grateful for having been invited to join the touring party. His divorce has just come through, and there's no prospect of a winter job, indeed of any future job at all. This is the world of Hamilton's *Pro* fifty years on.

Stott's inclusion in the tour has been at the insistence of its captain, Robin Barnett, a Varsity man, 'aloof and patrician' with the manner and bearing of Douglas Jardine, who travels with a copy of the *Financial Times* in his cricket bag. England's finest batter and long spoken of as a future captain, he'd been sent home from a previous tour of India when, in disgust at the tactics of his captain, he'd marched off the field in the middle of a test. This is why he's leading a motley crew in India rather than touring with the current English side in the West Indies.

Barnett's team has arrived in Madras for the culminating match of the tour. Not only has the umpire been murdered, but the city is caught up in a prolonged strike which has led to widespread unrest. The novel has a vivid sense of place and its brilliantly rendered crowd scenes, both on the streets and later at the cricket ground, provide a graphic setting for the world of baksheesh and corruption in which Stott soon finds himself entangled.

Sitting in the team's hotel bar late one evening, Stott is cornered by Barnett and Roy Cuthbert, a Midlands press baron known for his recent unsuccessful campaign to buy one of the nation's oldest football clubs and for having broken a printer's strike by bussing in non-union workers under the protection of armed security guards. Cuthbert has a proposal. Cricket, he says, is in a state of crisis. Spectators are bored. Cricketers can't earn the money they deserve or play the kind of cricket they'd enjoy. The problem, Cuthbert continues 'is the monopoly of the TCCB, the ICC, the MCC, the whole incestuous Lord's set-up'. His plan is to take up where Kerry Packer left off. Packer, he says, was only after television rights: 'Once he'd settled that, his series collapsed and his players returned to the fold, cap in hand'. Cuthbert, by contrast, intends to finance a new cricket league in England, Grand Prix Cricket.

Barnett fills in the details. Teams based in each major city and consisting of half local and half foreign players, matches to be played at converted football grounds, a one-day knockout cup and a four-day league. TV companies will come on board once the cricket monopoly is blown and then more sponsorship will follow. As will the big stars. It's all 'simply a question of money'.

Stott is partly convinced. Why should I, he wonders, 'stand shoulder to shoulder with the Moguls of the cricket establishment, safely ensconced in their clubhouses while the rest of us faced cold economic reality for the meagre reward of earning a basic living [...] There's a limit to how much you can enjoy a weekday afternoon spent chasing balls round an enormous field under the blank gaze of pensioners, dogs and little kids'.

But Stott is no star, and he wonders why they want to recruit someone like him. Barnett makes this brutally clear. It's because he's an old friend of Siva Ramachandran, the superstar of Indian cricket, a pin-up figure and an aspiring politician. Stott's friendship with Siva goes back 10 years to when they were young teammates in the same county side. Grand Prix Cricket depends on Siva: 'We need his talent. We need his charisma. We need his authority', explains Barnett. 'If Siva comes in, others will follow', adds Cuthbert. Stott, feeling 'like a fish struggling in a net', is to be the messenger.

He wakes next morning to the news that the umpire of the forthcoming match, an employee of the Commercial Trust Bank of Southern India, has been murdered, his skull speared with an old cricket stump. Pressured by Cuthbert and his captain, Stott visits Siva at his luxurious colonial mansion sheltered behind high white walls, large wrought-iron gates and set in a dense garden of mangoes, bananas, guavas and giant purple orchids looking down over the city. Siva, dressed in close-fitting, crisply creased white trousers, a gold-embroidered, open-necked shirt and pale buffalo leather sandals welcomes him. He encourages Stott to accept the offer of Grand Prix Cricket: 'Take Cuthbert's money [...] What do you owe Lord's or the TCCB or any of them?' Siva, however, has plans to stand for the State Legislature Assembly of Tamil Nadu. He wants to renew the Tamil Party by returning it to the people and resisting the power of Delhi. When leaving Siva's estate, Stott is assaulted and left barely in a fit state for the match that starts the next morning.

Chepauk Stadium is India's second-oldest test ground. The first test match to be played there was in 1934 against Douglas Jardine's touring England team. Currently home to the IPL team Chennai Super Kings, the ground is famous for its intense atmosphere and knowledgeable but passionate crowd. The description of it as seen through the bruised and swollen eyes of Stott on the first morning of the match is a fine set-piece:

> Men with steel trays packed with samosas or bhel pooris or ice creams or crisps or cucumber slices spread with lemon and chilli hawked their wares [...] Spectators filled not only all available seats but shimmied up poles and rafters and clung to the scoreboard. Tickets, of course, had multiplied several times in value as they were sold and resold [...] Cricket tickets are a special currency in India and there is not much you can't buy with them.

Their opponents are the strongest side Barnett's team has faced on the tour. The Indian selectors are using the match as a trial for an upcoming series against Australia, and the team is a mixture of rising young cricketers and established internationals. Foremost among the latter is their captain, the famed leg-spinner Chaughiri. Siva isn't playing, but when he appears at the ground shortly before the start, the crowd goes into uproar:

He was surrounded by an entourage of older men in suits and younger men in casual western dress: sweatshirts with lettering, plimsolls, creased denims. The crowd hailed him. He stood and returned their warmth […] as he turned and applauded his admirers, hands reaching high over his head.

The England team bats first, and after an early wicket, Barnett settles into his usual mode, scrupulously careful against good balls, elegantly severe on anything loose. From the dressing room balcony, looking down on his captain and the crowd, Stott notices Cuthbert sitting with Mr Narayan of the Commercial Trust Bank of Southern India, sponsor of the tour. Two rich men sitting together, he thinks, nothing very strange about that.

Stott comes to the wicket mid-afternoon after Barnett has been dismissed for a consummate century, emerging from the dressing room 'into the glare of the sun, the noise, and fifty thousand pairs of eyes'. The story of his assault has been headlined in the morning papers, his injuries are visible to the crowd, and to his embarrassment, he's applauded all the way to the crease. The square-leg umpire even shakes him by the hand.

Chaughiri is bowling. His first delivery, 'hovering (like) an apparently motionless bird […] hung in the air for ages, then dropped' and spun into his front pad. Avoiding Chaughiri as much as he can, Stott scrapes together a few runs. At each delivery he faces from the leg-spinner, the middle of his bat seems to shrink. He reflects on how hostile spin bowling can be: 'Its gentility, its sheer artful slowness, disguises aggression and violence'.

Suddenly, there's an interruption in the crowd. A spectator has climbed the wire fence and is holding a banner aloft, shouting fiercely in Tamil. A mob of police swiftly appears, drags the man and his banner down from his perch and frog-marches him away to both boos and cheers from the crowd. The noise subsides, but the atmosphere in the crowd remains seething. Stott asks Chaughiri what the incursion was about and is told the banner said, 'Release Imprisoned Strikers'.

Play resumes and Stott continues his struggle with the leg-spinner. Reaching the twenties and starting to feel more confident, he's deceived by a cleverly flighted ball which draws him into an attempted drive. The ball dips and swerves 'as if it had a life of its own', and he's left stranded, an easy stumping for the keeper.

Stott has been invited to a party at Siva's lavish home that evening. Leaving the grounds, he's accosted by Barnett reminding him to lobby Siva about Grand Prix Cricket. When Stott replies that Siva is going into politics and isn't interested, Barnett replies: 'He might be yet. Remind him of the Coromandel Coast Investments scheme'.

Stott is accompanied to the party by Lakshmi, a journalist investigating the murky world of Madras finance, cricket and politics who identifies the people around them, the inheritors of the British Raj as she calls them: 'The Black Raj. The Tamil Raj'. The room is abuzz with entitlement: oil importers, cigarette manufacturers, coir magnates, film producers, judges, all contributors to the Party and here to show support for Siva's political ambitions. Narayan is prominently among them, and so too is an Englishman, Shrapley – blue blazer, high open white collar, whisky in hand – a public school type Stott can imagine in the members' bar after a sunny day at Chelmsford or Taunton. Lakshmi identifies him as managing director of the plant at the centre of the strike. Any group wishing to take power in Madras, she explains, needs the support of the large foreign firms operating in the city. Shrapley's presence at the party has put his company's seal of approval on Siva's candidacy.

Behind the venal world Stott glimpses at the party, hinted at by Barnett's mention of the Coromandel Coast Investment Scheme (CCIS), is a South African connection. Stott's position on sport and apartheid is straightforward. Long ago, Siva had explained to him the reason for boycotting South African cricket, and out of respect for his friend he's remained loyal to the boycott, recently turning down an offer of winter work coaching in Western Provinces. Stott angrily rejects Lakshmi's suggestion that Siva's connection with Narayan and the Tamil party has compromised his friend's principled opposition to sporting contact with South Africa. A main thread of Marqusee's novel is the 'slow turn' in Stott's understanding of the emerging realities of world cricket in the 1980s.

Slow Turn opens with a prologue on the googly, how, contrary to appearances, it turns the wrong way. From the introduction of the CCIS, the novel, as any good crime story should, becomes as difficult to untangle as reading a googly. I shall try and explain. Marqusee incorporates the actual rebel tours of South Africa by English cricketers in 1982, and others by Sri Lankans, West Indians and Australians that followed, into the background of his novel. CCIS, we learn, is at the heart of South Africa's political project in the 1980s to end the boycott by provoking splits amongst the

Test-playing nations and undermining the international cricket establishment. Grand Prix Cricket is the next item on South Africa's agenda.

CCIS had been set up by a group of Indian businessmen in Durban made fabulously wealthy from profiteering during the Second World War. Investment from rich Tamil businessmen in Madras and capital from trading links with South African Breweries had enabled CCIS to finance rebel cricket tours and, now, Grand Prix Cricket.

When Siva returned to India after his apprenticeship in the county game, he was drawn into the political and financial circle of Narayan, who paid off his family debts and mentored his career with cheques drawn on the account of CCIS at the Commercial Trust Bank. But as Siva's wealth, fame and political plans grew, Narayan became resentful of his protégé's independence. These tensions, though not yet public, have left Siva, the people's champion, open to the risk of exposure by his mentor as being on the apartheid bankroll.

All this and much more is the setting against which the match at Chepauk Stadium is being played and where, in a climactic set-piece scene, the novel comes to its dramatic head. Lakshmi's investigations into Narayan and the CCIS are exposed in the Madras newspaper, *The Banner*. As news of the story spreads among the spectators, they riot. Fences are pulled up and thrown at the police who rush in to try and prevent a pitch invasion. Narayan is attacked. Tear gas is turned on the crowd. The riot is quelled only when Siva appears, arms aloft, signalling for peace. Anger turns to cheers. The people reach out to their hero. An uneasy calm returns, and the cricket is resumed.

Barnett and Stott are together at the crease. Barnett, realising his partner has had a hand in the disclosure, lets loose a drive aimed straight at Stott which he narrowly avoids. Trying to repeat the shot, Barnett is deceived by a perfectly concealed Chaughiri googly and bowled between bat and pad. Stott watches as his captain's 'erect carriage' disappears into the member's enclosure: 'It was the last I ever saw of him.' The old cricketer leaving the crease is a recurring figure in cricket fiction, but in the emergent world that *Slow Turn* has exposed it is no longer the end of the road.

Siva, compromised by his association with a corrupt world of finance and politics he has never fully understood, yet still the people's hero, announces his retirement from cricket and declares his candidacy for the State Legislative Assembly. Narayan is indicted for the murder of the umpire but never stands trial, a 'technicality' resulting in the charges being dropped. But he's been disgraced, and Siva, the new strongman of the Party, is elected to the State Assembly. Barnett moves to South Africa, where he continues to score masses of runs and becomes a popular figure. This 'old cricketer' has found a new and accommodating home. Cuthbert is untouched by the scandal. Stott is taken on by Barnett's old county, and Lakshmi turns her attention to investigating South African links with the English cricket establishment.

The whole thing, Stott concludes, 'was really a draw'. The project of Grand Prix Cricket has collapsed, and Stott's feeling after his midnight meeting with Barnett and Cuthbert that 'the old cricket structure seemed ready to crumble around my ears' has not yet been borne out. But *Slow Turn* perceptively understands and dramatises the politics and pressures which cricketers in the 1970s and 1980s were confronted with, and makes presciently clear where the game seems to be heading. The global dominance of sports capitalism, the novel suggests, will define the future of cricket.

The changing face of cricket exposed by Marqusee's novel was taken in new directions by Joseph O'Neill in his novel *Netherland* (2008), set in New York, much admired by Barack Obama, and influenced, I think, by several failed attempts in the years just before its publication to establish T20 franchise leagues in the United States.

Its opening scene is a cricket match on Staten Island a year after 9/11. We're at Randolph Walker Park, where the home team, made up of cricketers originating from Trinidad, Guyana, Jamaica, India, Pakistan and Sri Lanka, is playing against 'a bunch of guys from St Kitts – Kittitians'. The narrator, Hans van den Broek, a Dutch banker, is the only white man on the field.

Randolph Walker Park, as Hans describes it, is 'a very poor place for cricket'. The playing area is small, the outfield uneven and overgrown, and the pitch – made of clay and covered with coconut matting – of unreliable bounce. Nevertheless, it's an august venue. Staten Island Cricket Club was founded in 1872 and Don Bradman and Garry Sobers had both played there. Before play can begin, the teams have to wait for a softball match to clear the ground and for the Staten Island team – three Hindus, three Christians, a Sikh and four Muslims – to finish its prayer huddle. The Kittitian supporters line the boundary, drinking rum, eating barbecued red snapper and chicken and abusing the home umpire.

When one of the St Kitts bowlers, after letting loose a volley of bouncers, ignores the umpire's warning and delivers another throat-ball to Hans, the umpire rules he can no longer bowl. A row breaks out and a drunk St Kitts supporter comes onto the pitch with a gun. Players scatter. The umpire, assisted by the visiting captain, persuades the man to drop his gun and leave the field. Play resumes: 'Nobody sees any reason to call the cops'.

Several contrasting cricket scenes follow, backstories to this dramatic afternoon on Staten Island. The earliest is in The Hague. Cricket in Holland, Hans tells us, is played by a few thousand participants who go 'about their game with the seriousness and organisation that character-ises all Dutch sport', especially in The Hague where Dutch bourgeois snobbishness and cricket are a natural fit. From early childhood, Hans had played for the venerable team of Houdt Braef Standt (HBS), the club where his deceased father had played many years earlier. Although the HBS ground had a coconut matting wicket and its outfield, also used for winter games, was sluggish, it was worlds away from Randolph Walker Park. Hans has boyhood memories of lovely solitary cycle rides through the 'fragmented brilliance of the woods' in which the ground nestles, his red Gray-Nicolls bag resting on his handlebars, a lambswool sweater slung over his shoulders. His widowed mother would come to watch, sitting by the western sightscreen marking schoolwork and occasionally looking up to follow the game. The cricket itself, as it does elsewhere in the novel, prompts reflections of a more existential nature:

Your innings might be over in a second, as a life in eternity. Out, you trudge off miserably, irrevocably dismissed into the nothingness of the non-participant.

Flash forward a few years to South Bank Cricket Club in Herne Hill, London.

On marvellously shorn Surrey village greens – the smell of grass when mown in May provokes in me pangs of emotion that I still dare not dwell on – we battled gently for victory and drank warm beer on the steps of the ancient wooden pavilions.

The nostalgia of this scene – the 'sounds and rhythms of a full day's cricket, in which unhurried time is portioned out by the ticking of ball against bat' – is compounded by the absence of his mother. His wife Rachel, from whom he is separated for most of the novel, came once to watch and was bored silly by 'the green blankness' of it all. Cricket in Surrey, for all its enchantment, is full of absences. Memory, for Hans, is always the ache of things that have passed.

Hans's return to cricket in New York is a side-effect of 9/11 and the subsequent departure of Rachel to London, taking their young son with her. He digs out his cricket gear, untouched for years, from the storage unit where his and Rachel's possessions have been kept since they were forced to move after the terrorist attack. It's all there, his old kit, in the black hole of a Duncan Fearnley bag:

> (T)he Slazenger Viv Richards batting pads with stuffing leaking from the seams; thick-fingered, sweat-darkened batting gloves; unwashed white socks; an anti-erotic jockstrap; and my HBS sweater, moth-eaten and shrunken [...] I pulled out my old bat. It was more cracked than I remembered. The traces of long-gone cricket balls still reddened its blade. I gripped the worn rubber-sleeved handle with bare hands and crouched into a batting stance. Seeing a fast half-volley land by some boxed books, I strode with my left foot to the pitch of the ball and dreamily smashed it.

It's a splendid passage, the archaeology of a disused cricket bag, the run of compound adjectives contrasting vividly with the hazy, generic description of cricket in Herne Hill while evoking its own sweaty nostalgia. Hans gathers up his bag and sets off for Staten Island and the resumption of his cricket career.

But returning to the game is never easy, whether after a long absence or even just at the beginning of a new season. Hans is 34 and troubled by backache:

> Throwing a ball is harder than we remember [...] The ball itself feels very hard: skyers struck in catching practice are a little frightening. Bats that were light and wand-like when picked up fantastically during the off-season are now heavy and spade-like. Running between the wickets leaves us breathless. Trotting and bending down after a moving ball hurts body parts we'd thought renewed by months of rest. We have not succeeded, we discover, in imagining out of existence cricket's difficulties.

O'Neill here captures a feeling familiar to any cricketer past the flush of youth.

Cricket in *Netherland*, for all the finesse with which its details are rendered, is woven into the novel's pervasive sense of loss: the loss of Hans' past and of his wife and son; his solitary existence in the Chelsea Hotel (haunt of writers, musicians and artists, where Sid and Nancy lived and Nancy was murdered); and the loss of meaning in his life. The marginal world of New York cricket, of New York immigrants and a post-9/11 city whose collective memory is permeated with loss and fear, is brilliantly rendered both in its own right and as a correlative of Hans' numbed state of mind and being. But cricket can also provide a comfort of sorts, a ghetto offering some kind of continuity with a migrant's past.

This latter note is memorably struck in the last of the novel's descriptions of an actual cricket setting. Poughkeepsie (the name itself somehow conveys a sense of comfort and joy) is the furthest north of the grounds the Staten Island team visits. On the outskirts of the town, a colony of Jamaicans has maintained a cricket field on a 'lush hillside'. The batting track was made of cement, 'bouncy but true': 'If you smashed the ball down the hill it landed among cows, goats, horses, chickens.' Inevitably, there was an umpiring row but after the match, the players gathered in the clubhouse, where signs warned against the use of marijuana, to enjoy a meal of chicken and rice while around them solemn games of dominoes were being played. Hans rhapsodises the scene: 'The tilted pretty cricket ground, the shipshape clubhouse – such pioneering effort had gone into them.'

Let's back up a bit. The umpire that day on Staten Island who disarmed the Kittitian is Chuck Ramkissoon, a Trinidadian entrepreneur with whom Hans falls into a kind of friendship. Chuck has a big idea, a sports arena for the greatest cricket teams in the world, 12 exhibition matches every summer at a venue to include tennis, squash, tenpin bowling, a gymnasium, swimming pool, a sports bar and restaurant, but with cricket at its centre. 'Think global TV rights for a game in New York City between India and Pakistan', he tells Hans. Chuck meets Hans' bemused scepticism with a blizzard of stats about the changing demography of New York: nearly a million English-speaking West Indians; an Indian population that has grown 81 per cent in the last decade, the Pakistani population by 150 per cent in the same period and Bangladeshis by 500 per cent; almost half a million South Asians in the city and their numbers expanding rapidly in New Jersey. And, he insists, they haven't just come to mop floors and drive taxis. They've come to make 'real money' in hi-tech, pharmaceuticals, electronics, healthcare. And their children are playing cricket everywhere in the city:

> They play at Dutch Kills Playground [...] they play in vacant lots, they play in schoolyards up and down Queens and Brooklyn [...] you'll see boys and girls with cricket bats, even in the snow. If I took you there now, I could show you the wicket they've drawn on the wall.

Nor, Chuck insists, is cricket just an immigrant activity. It was America's first modern team sport. As always, he has facts at his fingertips. The game has been played in New York since the 1770s. The first-ever international team-sports fixtures were cricket matches between the United States of America and Canada in the 1840s and 1850s, watched by thousands of fans. There were clubs all over the country from Boston to San Francisco, Kentucky to Philadelphia. 'Cricket is already in the American DNA'.

He takes Hans to the proposed site, Floyd Bennett Field, Brooklyn, a disused airfield: 'I have the land, I have the lease, I have the backing', Chuck tells him. He's going to name it Bald Eagle Field: 'It's got scale. It makes it American'. It also pays homage to the eagles and other birdlife that inhabit the setting, and to the migrating species which pass over the field on their Atlantic flyway. Birds are a recurring figure of transitoriness, and sometimes of captivity, throughout the novel. Hans gazes at the winter landscape: 'Under the snow, I was being asked to believe, lay the finest, most fragile area of grass known to sports: a cricket square'.

Some months later Chuck takes Hans back to Bald Eagle Field, now transformed into a bright green playing field. Chuck goes down on his knees and spreads his hands over the shortened grass 'like a hallower'. The pitch is being rolled, the outfield mowed. Chuck's dream is starting to be realised. He tells Hans of how, as a kid back in Trinidad, his local club, Las Lomas, had ploughed up the recreation ground and made it into a proper cricket field, how he'd listened in the club shed to broadcasts of Frank Worrell's West Indian team in Australia in 1960–1961, how he'd learnt the language of cricket from commentators like John Arlott and how from a small shed in Trinidad he'd learnt of the wider world of cricket. Chuck's vision of an arena originates from a world of long ago and far away.

O'Neill has spoken of his novel as 'having some kind of a conversation with *The Great Gatsby*'. The relation of O'Neill's reserved but observant narrator, Hans, to the exuberant and enterprising Chuck parallels that of

Scott Fitzgerald's narrator, Nick Carraway, to Jay Gatsby. Both novels are set in New York, and both critically examine the 'American Dream' of the United States as a place of unlimited opportunity for the incomer. Gatsby, from North Dakota, and Chuck, from Trinidad, are versions appropriate to their period of the outsider making good. Their success, however, has murky foundations and eventually crumbles to nothing. The world of each novel is, of course, very different. One of Fitzgerald's main characters, Tom Buchanan, a former Yale football star, asserts the superiority of the Nordic races and is hostile to immigration. New York is now a place of immigrants and their children, a global city. Chuck, nevertheless, will end up dead in a ditch.

O'Neill described *Netherland* as a farewell to the world of *The Great Gatsby*, 'a post-American novel' as he puts it. It is also a post-colonial novel in which a black immigrant entrepreneur sets out like Kerry Packer a quarter of a century earlier to exploit the global possibilities of cricket. Hans, intrigued by the vision, his relationship with his wife and son draining away, becomes Chuck's assistant groundsman. Each weekend, at the end of a morning's work at the field, they stand at the wicket and whack balls to every part of the ground, studying the pace and consistency of the outfield, after which Chuck drives Hans to wherever he is playing that day: 'Our field and those fields were [...] one continuum of heat and greenness'.

Time passes, and Hans comes to see that Chuck's vision is a fantasy. The two men grow distant. Hans returns to England and is uneasily reunited with Rachel and his son. The novel loops back to where it started with a phone call from a *New York Times* reporter telling Hans that Chuck has been found dead in the Gowanus Canal, handcuffed and evidently murdered. The Canal is in Long Island, Gatsby territory, notorious for its pollution and where the Mafia is said to dump bodies. With the narrative of Chuck and Hans now complete – the novel is essentially one long flashback with a series of shorter internal flashbacks – Hans goes to Google Maps and revisits Bald Eagle Field: 'There's Chuck's field. It is brown – the grass has burned [...] There's no trace of a batting square. The equipment shed is gone. I'm just seeing a field'. The dream has come to nothing.

Netherland extends a traditional interest in cricket fiction – how the game offers a home, a sense of identity and shared purpose, pleasure or consolation – to a non-traditional setting and to a body of cricketers living far from home creating sub-communities of their own. The idea of New York as a city of cricket is striking, demographically savvy and culturally fascinating. Here it is a game of migrants, a place of sanctuary for the Dutchman, Hans, as well as for those from the Caribbean, India, Pakistan and Sri Lanka he plays alongside. All those on this 'patch of America sprinkled with the foreign-born strangely at play [...] are far away from Tipperary, and clubbing together mitigates this unfair fact'.

But as well as the idea of cricket as a home away from home, or Chuck's vision of cricket as part of America's destiny, it is also something distinct from place, culture or history. Hans has a more universal vision of the game.

> [I]t's my belief that the communal contractual phenomenon of New York cricket is underwritten, there where the print is finest, by the same agglomeration of unspeakable individual longings that under-writes cricket played anywhere – longings [...] that touch on the undoing of losses too private and reprehensible to be acknowledged to oneself, let alone to others. I cannot be the first to wonder if what we see, when we see men in white take to a cricket field, is men imag-ining an environment of justice.

It's a complex passage suggesting that another reason people play cricket is because of a shared psychology, some underlying oneness intrinsic to the game that its participants and followers bring with them to the sport. It is this, the novel in its entirety implies, that lies behind Hans's return to cricket when his wife and son depart for England, behind Chuck's big idea, behind everyone else's reason for playing it and behind the power of cricket to generate passion and become an obsession.

Overriding all this, or perhaps cannily exploiting it in the way that capitalism does, is the emerging reality of cricket in the twenty-first cen-tury. Chuck's initial backer was a multimillionaire, multimedia guru and cricket nut, Faruk Patel, a shadowy figure until Hans meets him towards the end of the novel. The problem with Chuck's New York Cricket Club scheme, he tells Hans, was his obsession with America. America is unnec-essary and irrelevant, Patel explains: 'You have the TV, internet markets' – put the stadium up and you're done with America. Cricket doesn't need to be rooted anywhere. Chuck's American Dream was already anachro-nistic and irrelevant, unsustainable by any one person, even a major ven-ture capitalist like Patel. Cricket is global, a major player in the world of media capitalism and international finance, part of a worldwide network of fabulously wealthy overlapping and competing interests.

In this respect, *Netherland* is remarkably prescient. American Major League Cricket (MLC), the latest international T20 league competition, began in 2023 in a converted baseball stadium in Dallas. It has the financial backing of leading Indian American tech executives such as the Microsoft chief executive and is supported by four IPL franchises and two state cricketing bodies from Australia as owners or partners of its six founding teams. It has recruited an impressive mix of current stars – Steve Smith, Glenn Maxwell, Kagiso Rabada and Pat Cummins, for example; recent retirees and veterans such as Quinton de Kock, Aaron Finch and Trent Boult; and celebrated former internationals, among them Stephen Fleming, Lasith Malinga and Shane Watson, as coaches.

The 2024 International Cricket Council (ICC) T20 World Cup, co-hosted by the United States and the West Indies, was an updated version of Chuck's dream as reimagined by Faruk Patel. Three U.S. venues, the showpiece a pop-up 34,000-seater stadium on Long Island with a drop-in pitch, where India and Pakistan met in the first group stage. Chuck's vision of millions of viewers worldwide watching these two rivals meet in New York in front of the city's cricket-loving ex-pat communities became a reality, with India calling most of the shots. The ICC's broadcast deal for the T20 World Cup was £2.3 billion, with the Indian TV market contributing 90 per cent of the revenue. The 2028 Olympic Games, at which T20 cricket will feature, will be a further step in this process, its three hours of non-stop action ideal for global viewing and hugely profitable when the TV rights are sold. India will again be the major beneficiary.

Netherland leaves open the question of whether cricket's more traditional forms will survive, but for Hans at least the prospect seems gloomy. Back in London and reunited with his family, he wonders if he still needs his cricket bat. He hesitates: 'to throw out this odd paddle would [...] go against nature, even though its wood [...] is now swollen with age and cannot have a sweet spot to speak of'. O'Neill has a fine eye for detail, and the recurring appearances of Hans' cricket bat in *Netherland* carry memories and tell stories (like a very humble domestic version of the stories embedded in Tam's bat in *Half of the Human Race*). But by the end of the novel, these memories and stories are fading, and he realises that his bat embodies 'something essentially nostalgic'. When Rachel asks if he's going to play again this year, he replies he doesn't think so. He shows the bat to his son, Luke, remembering as he does 'the white flashes of boys mysteriously organised in a green space' in a wood on the edge of The

Hague, his father's old ground. Luke, engrossed in watching *Jurassic Park*, isn't interested. Hans is unexpectedly relieved. Cricket, as he has known it, has lost its sweet spot. There's no 'young-un' pointing to the future in *Netherland*. Rather than the son dragging his father out to practice his cricket, as happens at the close of De Sélincourt's *The Cricket Match*, in *Netherland* the father's suggestion is rejected by the son. O'Neill's novel is not only a farewell to Gatsby and the American Dream but also, it seems, to the time-honoured worlds of traditional cricket and those generational ties that have, in the past, secured its continuity.

And yet the story of the 2024 T20 World Cup, surprisingly, might suggest otherwise. The original New York venue selected by the ICC, Van Cortlandt Park in the Bronx, a more central location than Long Island, was strongly resisted by the local cricket leagues. Eight cricket fields would have been lost, and the ICC's promise to restore and upgrade them after the World Cup was mistrusted. As the current president of the Staten Island Cricket League put it: the ICC 'will pack up, take their money and leave the repairs to New York's parks department, on the taxpayer's dime'. Local politicians argued that the plan violated the New York public trust doctrine that parks may only be used for public enjoyment, and in the end the ICC gave way. New York's 150-year-old tradition of communal and recreational forms of cricket will persist, enhanced by its very different present-day cultural make-up.

Shehan Karunatilaka's *Chinaman* is another cricket novel with an international setting – Sri Lanka, in this case. Part mystery novel, part comedy, part tragedy, part family drama and memoir, *Chinaman* is a virtuosic blend of realism with the absurd and fantastic set in the modern cricket world of illicit, often foolish betting, bribes and kickbacks, match-fixing and sex, and drawing almost anything you can think of into its orbit.

Where best to start? Perhaps with its five-part structure and the parallel this creates between the novel and a test match – First Innings, Second Innings, Close of Play, Follow On, Last Over. But within this outer frame, the novel shifts backwards and forwards, cutting here and there, turning this way and that. Reading it can feel like you're a batter trying to decipher the bewildering variations of the mystery spinner at its heart. As I try to write about it, I'm caught in its toils.

Better therefore to start with its narrator. Whereas O'Neill's narrator is reticent, scrupulous, almost passive, as reflected in the muted, elegant style of the novel, Karunatilaka's is an extrovert, exuberant, unreliable, frank, though not always truthful, and the style of his narrative is correspondingly energetic and demotic. W. G. Karunasena is a 64-year-old alcoholic cricket writer who wishes he were known by his initials, 'like T.S. Eliot, D.H. Lawrence. Even O.J. Simpson'. His full name is Wijedasa Gamini Karunasena. His mother and sisters call him Sudu; his wife calls him Gamini; his friends, Wije; strangers, Karunasena; and his brothers no longer call him at all. He's named his own son Garfield, playing on the old joke that Sobers was never sober and W.G. lacked grace. I shall honour his wish and call him W.G.

His narrative opens with the question: 'Why [...] has no one heard of our nation's greatest cricketer?' The man in question is Pradeep Mathew, a left-arm mystery spinner who has disappeared and whose test record has been erased and forgotten. W.G. thinks of him as the 'great unsung bowler', just as he thinks of Sri Lanka as 'the great underachieving nation' and himself as 'the great unfulfilled writer'. Everything about Pradeep Mathew is mysterious: his origins, upbringing, early career, test record, disappearance, even whether he's alive or dead. His sister claims he's dead, but is she really his sister? Did Mathew even have a sister? The whole novel is like this, a quest narrative in which W.G.'s search for Mathew is met with false trails, dead-ends, wrong turnings and red herrings. For most of its length, *Chinaman* is a wild goose chase. Marqusee's prologue on the googly as an emblem of mystery has become the subject of a major cricket novel.

WG's starting point is that Mathew must be the finest test bowler of all time because his record of 47 wickets in 7 matches far outdoes that of any other. He provides a comparative table of wickets per match – Botham 3.75, Hadlee 5.01, Imran 4.11, Kapil 3.31 – to establish his case. It's odd, perhaps, that there's no mention here of Muttiah Muralitharan, whose average of just over six wickets per test match was sealed with his 800th test wicket, taken with the final delivery of his career, a neat reversal of Bradman's failure to score the four runs he needed in his final test to retire with a batting average of 100.

W.G. first saw Mathew in action in a test match between Sri Lanka and Pakistan at the Tyronne Cooray Stadium in Asgiriya in 1986. The ground, no longer used for test cricket, was named after a Sri Lankan politician who'd fought, lobbied and cajoled the ICC in his efforts to win Sri Lanka test status: 'That failed. He then tried wining, dining and bribing. That worked'. W.G., badly hung-over after passing the night under a bo tree, like the Buddha he remarks, is watching Mathew bowling in the nets. Something is amiss: 'Mathew, left-arm chinaman bowler, is bowling with his right arm, in the style of the opposing spin wizard, Abdul Qadir. The mimicry is spot on'. As W.G. watches, Mathew switches to his left arm off a longer run and reproduces a perfect copy of Wasim Akram shattering the wickets with a yorker. Imitations of every Pakistani bowler follow: Imran, Zakir and the sideways delivery skip of Mudassar Nazar.

His next sight of Matthew is at a test at the same ground between Sri Lanka and New Zealand the following year, a match that almost never happened and officially never did. Shortly before the match, a car bomb had exploded at the Colombo central bus station, killing 113 people and injuring hundreds more. The New Zealanders immediately packed their bags and prepared to fly home, but the match was saved by the pleadings of the politician after whom the stadium had been named. It helped that he had secured a virtual monopoly of the local milk powder market for the large New Zealand exporter, Anchor.

W.G. tells us that he's only seen real beauty twice in his life:

Sixty-four years, two things of beauty. One I have failed to cherish, the other I might yet be able to.

Sheila at the Galle Face Hotel, 31st Nite Dinner Dance, 1963.
PS Mathews vs New Zealand at Asgiriya, 1987.

Sheila is W.G.'s feisty, long-suffering wife. Mathew's record spell in 1987 – 'the finest spell of spin bowling or any bowling on this or any other planet, that I or anyone else could ever have seen' – 10-51, two runs better than Jim Laker's record – has, like the match itself, been expunged: 'Today there is no record of the record, even in *Wisden*'.

At the start of play, the pavilion was filled with politicians and VIPs, but the rest of the stadium was empty. The few journalists allowed into the press box had been told their match reports would need the approval of the government censor. At lunch, New Zealand were 73-2, Crowe Jr and Turner, 'the wine and cheese man and the beer and pie man', having scored freely. Mathew had taken the two wickets to fall, his lunchtime figures reading 2-47.

It's after lunch that W.G. has his second vision of 'staggering beauty'. Crowe Jr is the first to go, bowled attempting to cut a chinaman, followed by Crowe Sr and Evan Gray who fall to Mathew's boru ball (we're never actually told what this is). Turner is deceived by Mathew's undercutter but survives. Next ball, he's struck in the face by a medium-paced leaper. He advances down the pitch towards Mathew and has to be restrained. Carrom flicks and darters account for Hadlee, Bracewell and Snedden. Then Mathew bowls his supreme delivery. It pitches wide of leg like a mis-placed carrom ball, spins towards the off stump, then darts back towards the wickets: 'The double bounce ball, cricket's most magnificent creation'. Turner shouts to the dressing room, 'This pitch is fucked!' Mathew repeats the delivery and the ball takes Turner's middle stump. New Zealand has slumped from 111 for 2 to 117 all out. After tea, they refuse to take the field. Discussions follow, the pitch is deemed unsuitable, the match abandoned and the three sessions of play declared null and void. Any paper publish-ing a match report will have its licence revoked. The test was wiped from the record and so too was Mathew's record bowling spell.

Chinaman is a book for bowlers, packed with descriptions of Mathew's novel variations and illustrated with spidery little sketches, like a Ronald Searle doodle, to show what a chinaman, a lissa, a floater and a carrom flick are. Only the boru goes unillustrated. These depictions are often supplemented with little stories, some fanciful, others not, explaining the origin of a particular style. The first of these is the overarm delivery itself, which, we're told, was introduced in the colonies several centuries ago when the ladies at charity amusements found their hoop dresses made underarm bowling impossible, and so they invented overarm bowling. Another is the term 'Chinaman', reliably said to derive from when Walter Robins, an English captain in the 1930s, was dismissed by such a delivery from a West Indian bowler of Chinese descent and exclaimed: 'Fancy being done by a bloody Chinaman'. W.G. and his cricketing companion Ari debate the use of the term. Ari insists it's racist; W.G., ever the con-trarian, defends it by claiming that Conrad and Agatha Christie had used it too.

Comparisons with other mystery spinners are also part of the story. The lissa, or flipper, for example, was invented by Clarrie Grimmett but augmented by Mathew developing a ball that not only skidded but also changed direction. Jack Iverson's carrom flick – 'bending his middle finger as if he were flicking a leech off the ball' – is another. And not to forget the lob. In Zimbabwe in 1994, at the 'twilight of his career', Mathew was no-balled for a delivery that 'flew some 20 feet skywards before bouncing on the wickets'. The umpire deemed it illegal for 'hanging in the air too long'.

But best of all is the delivery without a precursor: 'The mystery of mystery balls. A ball that bounces and changes direction *twice*. A 5 ounce, spherical leather-bound object made to behave like a pebble skimming water'. As if to highlight the sublime absurdity of this delivery, the immediately following section, 'Scorpion Kick', is a hallucinatory cricket scene, like something from the croquet match in *Alice in Wonderland*, in which the score decreases from 400 for 5 to 210 for 7 and Mathew faces the bowling of Kerry Packer. Others appearing in this dream sequence are Sid Barnes, Jack Iverson, David Bairstow and Justin Fashanu, each of whom committed suicide; the former All Black rugby captain, Buck Shelford, who had his scrotum ripped open and a testicle left hanging after being rucked by a French boot (the tear was stitched up and Shelford returned to the field); George Best and Douglas Jardine, a disturbing assemblage of sportsmen that brings to the surface a dark thread which is part of the weft of the novel. But true to its rich tapestry, relief is provided by the Colombian goalkeeper, Rene Higuita, preventing a six by scorpion-kicking the ball back into play, and the Chaplinesque figure of Derek Randall walking out to bat followed by a butcher with a wheelbarrow of pork chops.

This scene, becoming curiouser and curiouser, is an intensification of *Chinaman's* signature note in which the real is blended with the fictive to create a kind of in-between world. Elsewhere we learn that Mathew is (or was?) triple-jointed: able to remove his sweater by reaching behind his right hip with his left hand, touch his elbow with his middle finger and open a bottle of Fanta with two bent fingers and a thumb. Otherwise, he wouldn't have been able to bowl his floater, his skidder or his double bounce ball. We're imaginatively willing to suspend our disbelief at the unlikelihood of all this, but we're also shown a muted black-and-white photo of a left-arm spinner, purportedly Mathew, bowling with an action in which shoulder, elbow and wrist are twisting in different directions, as if imitating the track of his legendary double bounce ball. Other semi-darkened photos include family shots implied to be of Mathew's own and the scoreboard at Tyronne Cooray Stadium recording a match in which Mathew, we can just make out through the murk of the photo, has taken 9 for 40. The effect of these pictures is to provide a questionable documentary realism for the unlikely or the impossible.

The reason, I think, that Muralitharan isn't included in W.G.'s table of wickets per test is because he figures in the novel as a kind of avatar of Mathew, his reincarnation. There's a shadowy photo of Mathew early in the novel which could be mistaken for Murali, and their association is firmly established in the closing scene of Part One, 'First Innings'. W.G. and Ari are watching Murali on TV, bowling against South Africa in Cape Town. W.G. is in raptures at the sight of Muralitharan's 'wrist flapping in the wind, unleashing curling deliveries that drop just out of the batsman's reach and turn at impossible angles […] While he may not quite have the genius of Mathew, he appears to have a discipline over his art that eluded Mathew'. Otherwise the game is dull, and the two indulge in their favourite pastime of selecting Sri Lanka's greatest-ever team. Ari excludes Murali because he thinks he chucks. W.G. is incandescent, and an ugly argument breaks out, which ends with W.G. sprawled on the floor, clutching his abdomen, and being taken off to the hospital with liver collapse. When Ari visits him in the hospital, his friend enmeshed in 'tubes attempting to pump death' from his body, the argument starts up again. Ari holds his ground; W.G. insists that it's Murali's wrist that turns, 'not the bloody elbow', that it's 'an optical illusion' (a bit like the novel as a whole).

The following part of *Chinaman*, 'Second Innings', concludes with a parallel scene, though with much wider implications. It is 21 January 1999. W.G. and Ari are again watching cricket on TV, Sri Lanka versus England. The Sri Lankan government has just killed 17 Tigers. Sri Lanka's long and bloody civil war shadows the cricket throughout. The square-leg umpire, the Australian Ross Emerson, no balls Murali and points to his elbow. Ari says he knew this would happen. The Sri Lankan captain, Arjuna Ranatunga, furious, approaches the umpire, his finger wagging. In cricket, the unprecedented always happens twice. Twelve years earlier, another fat and angry captain, the Englishman Mike Gatting, had confronted the Pakistan umpire Shakoor Rana in identical fashion. W.G. and Ari resume their argument. Ranatunga switches Murali to Emerson's end and insists the umpire stand up to the stumps, which means he can't see if the elbow is straightening. W.G. is ecstatic at this act of brazenness and wishes that Mathew had had such a captain to defend him. The match goes down to the wire, 'Mr Muttiah Murali, the man most sinned against, the second greatest bowler Sri Lanka has ever produced', Mathew's avatar, hitting the winning run. In Hindi and Urdu, 'doosra' means the second or the other one.

Let's cut to the wild goose chase. A piece W.G. has written on Sri Lanka's 10 greatest cricketers is taken up as a project for a TV documentary series. He fights long and hard to have Mathew included, every step of the way a maze of intrigue and obstruction. Eventually, W.G. gets his way, and on the night of the transmission, he gathers around the screen with Ari and others involved in making the film. The opening title comes up: 'Sri Lanka's Finest' followed by 'Pradeep Mathew. The Mystery', and then the voice-over – 'Why did Pradeep Mathew only play four tests? Why did he never blossom into greatness? The answer can be summed up in one word [...]' And then the lights go out: 'The image on the TV collapses like a dead star. We sit in darkness, pupils dilating [...] waiting, hoping for it only to be a short power-cut, but knowing it won't be'. Indeed it isn't. The cuts go on for months, the documentary is lost, 'and I, W. G. Karunasena, sit in the darkness and drink'.

W.G.'s fascination with Mathew, now an obsession, becomes a book project, and his search for the vanished bowler continues against the background of civil war and the big money, sleaze and corruption of Sri Lankan cricket. This takes W.G. down many strange paths, among them his pursuit of a rumoured six-fingered bowling coach said to have taught Mathew his tricks. W.G. meets a journalist who claims to have coached Mathew at school and does indeed have a huge scar between the thumb and forefinger of his left hand, which he claims, marks where his extra finger used to be. He also claims that Sobers was born with an extra finger on each hand, both of which were removed at birth. Like other implausible leads, these take W.G. no closer to the cricketer with whom he is obsessed but give substance to the strange, corrupt, violent and absurd world of Sri Lankan cricket and politics through which he stumbles.

W.G., in his contrary way, insists he is no racist: 'Sinhalese, Tamils, Muslims and Burghers all nauseate me in equal measure'. He blames some of the responsibility for Sri Lanka's racial problems on the British, but insists that by the 1950s, there was no need for outside help in fomenting the tensions that exploded into civil war. Mathew was Tamil, 'cursed for his race and his temperament' as W.G. puts it. As a cricket coach declares, 'Tamils have to be twice as good as Sinhalese to be recognised'. Mathew most certainly was, which resulted in him being recruited by a leading public school, Royal, nursery of many Sri Lankan test cricketers, to play in their annual matches with other top schools, contests that W.G. compares to Eton versus Harrow. These guest appearances, he discovers, were made in disguise, his darker skin camouflaged with sunscreen and his bowling style varying according to the requirements of the match. From his early years, Mathew had multiple identities.

Mathew was an outsider by temperament as well as class and ethnicity. He's a difficult man. His enthusiasm for cricket fluctuates. He writes poems to his girlfriend. In the 1986 home series against Pakistan, he ignores the SLBCC directive that certain rules were to be bent and loses his place in the team. The independence and outsider status of W.G.'s lost hero is the reason he played so little, disappeared so easily, and why the records of his cricket career have mysteriously vanished with him.

W.G. eventually learns the story of when, how and why Mathew vanished from Reggie Ranwala, one of the many groupies and hangers-on who inhabit the sleazy world of Sri Lankan cricket. It was 1995, and the Sri Lankan team on tour in New Zealand had just won its first-ever overseas test match. There had been a party in the hotel suite of the director of the Sri Lankan board of cricket, Jayantha Punchipala, 'filled with every Sri Lankan south of Papua New Guinea'. Hours after the management of the Wellington Inter-Continental had closed down the raucous celebrations, Reggie woke up lying on the floor behind a couch, 'curled up next to a pot plant, carpet burn on his face', to overhear Mathew accusing Punchipala of creaming off the proceeds of the tour, complicity in the assassination of a government minister and demanding the director hands over his fee for the tour, NZ$278,000. The furious director tells Mathew he'll never play cricket anywhere ever again. Sri Lanka's records are being computerised and his brother-in-law's San Francisco firm has the contract for this: 'I will erase you. Every wicket you've taken will no longer exist. In ten years no one will remember you'. Mathew takes the cheque and disappears from the record. W.G. remarks that if his 'stack of tall stories now resembles the Manhattan skyline, then let this last one be its Empire State'. Except that this story has the ring of truth.

Mysteries are invariably more interesting than their solution. At the end of the third part, 'Follow On', W.G. dies. But before he does, he's reunited with his long-estranged son, Garfield, an errant musician, and meets his young grandson, Jimi, named not after Hendrix, Page or even Laker, but James Jamerson, 'the finest bass to walk the earth' and who, like Mathew, no one remembers. As this suggests, and the title of the fourth part, Follow On, confirms, the scene is set for the father's quest to be taken over by his son. *Chinaman* is another cricket story of fathers and sons.

Garfield, who now goes by the name of the novel's author, Shehan, picks up the scent where his father had lost it, in New Zealand, and eventually solves the mystery of the missing mystery spinner. He is led to it when he comes across a young lad playing cricket on a beach who bowls a ball that bounces and spins twice, the final clue.

I'm not sure the novel quite survives the death of W.G. and the loss of his voice. Shehan writes the book of Mathew that his father never managed, but at the suggestion of his agent, he reframes it as a novel rather than a documentary. The SLBCC threatens legal action, but as the agent says, the market for 'true fiction from South Asia has become international [...] cricket and the subcontinent are very much in', adding that getting sued would be good for sales. The book is taken on by an American publisher and released under the surname of Karunatilaka. And so we come full metafictional circle. The book you've just finished is the story of the writing of the book. Although true to the topsy-turvy spirit of *Chinaman* in its mixing of the fictive and the real, the wit and vitality of W.G.'s voice, which has sustained this intermingling, are rather lost in the interests of bringing the magical mystery tour to an end.

But at its best, that is for more than three-quarters of its length, *Chinaman* is like nothing ever before attempted in cricket fiction. In many ways, it reminds me of Laurence Sterne's *Tristram Shandy*, published in the 1760s at the very moment the novel was becoming a distinct form, a work that playfully and seriously defied the emerging conventions of fiction even as they were being established. Cricket has taken much longer to produce anything similar.

These two novels, published 250 years apart, have many things in common. They share an absurdist love of experiment, including inventiveness with the printed text itself, and the book as a physical object. *Tristram Shandy* has a double-sided page that is entirely black, another entirely marbled, and one in which, when Corporal Trim flourishes his stick, the action is described not in words but by a twirling line on the page. In a parallel manner, *Chinaman* incorporates photographs of the fictive, including a scoreboard masquerading as genuine, and diagrams of Mathew's coiling and turning variations that even look rather like Corporal Trim's squiggly flourish.

Karunatilaka shares Sterne's playfulness with language, particularly with the length of Sri Lankan names, describing his country as 'the land of long names, long waits and long promises'. My favourite is the Sri Lankan fielder, Pushpakumara, who throws the ball at Turner's head. Ravindra Pushpakumara played 23 tests for Sri Lanka and was later the bowling coach of the national team, but kumara is also the name of New Zealand's native sweet potato. Punchipala, director of the SLBCC, the 'powerbroker [...] with the iron fist', is another such portmanteau word. Ellewellekankanage Asoka de Silva is presented to us as real, but who knows.

Both novelists love to digress and to send their readers down long winding trails. The one batter Mathew could never bamboozle was the Zimbabwean, Anton Rose, a man with 'five or six different shots' for each ball – the almost undismissible batter meeting the almost unplayable bowler. He's another Mathew analogue, but whereas we know Murali to have been real, Rose's status is a tease, plausibly presented in terms indistinguishable from the many actual cricketers inhabiting the novel. W.G. possesses his biography, *The Great Anton Rose* by Booth Beckman, and Rose himself figures in the long list of acknowledgements at the back of the book alongside cricket writers and luminaries such as Ed Smith, Mike Marqusee and Laurence Booth. So I went on a wild goose chase of my own in search of Beckman's book – replicating W.G.'s quest for Mathew – to discover that Booth Beckman was a little-known author of speculative and literary fiction with no cricket titles to his credit (a friend of the author's perhaps?).

The deepest resemblance between *Tristram Shandy* and *Chinaman* is the theme of obsession. Every character in Sterne's novel is dominated by a ruling passion, a 'hobby-horse' as the novel describes it. Tristram's Uncle Toby, for example, having been wounded in the groin at the siege of Namur during the Nine Years' War, has retired to a life of obsessive attention to the history and science of military fortifications. W.G. and Ari's obsession is cricket. They live it, fight over their differing memories of its past and their opinions of its contemporary condition, hurling batteries of statistics, real and fake, at each other to support their passionate contentions. The comedy of the novel, and of W.G.'s search for Mathew, rests on the idea that nothing matters so much as cricket except perhaps, as W.G. occasionally concedes, Sri Lanka's civil war.

Although absurd, this is rarely mocked. Just as Uncle Toby's hobby-horse provides psychological relief from his emasculating wound, so too the friends' obsession with cricket ministers to many important needs, extending from a deep concern with the state of their nation to the question of how they should best live their lives or compensate for its failures.

Perhaps no other sport can quite do this. Or, at least if its fiction is anything to go by, the game has a plenitude of followers who ride their hobby-horse for similar reasons.

Ultimately, the brilliance of *Chinaman* rests on how it captures and expands our understanding of cricket and its relation to the contemporary world – in a work whose very form mirrors a five-day cricket test – by putting the reader in the position of a batter struggling with a mystery bowler. Form and theme, manner and matter, are a perfect fit. Grappling with the book, I've sometimes felt like the wicketkeeper who devised a system with Mathew to help him read the spinner's bewildering variations. Mathew painted the index and ring fingers of his right (non-bowling) hand with 'some Hindu powder from the kovil'. The painted fingers would indicate the direction of the spin, the unpainted ones the length. In the end, it proved too much for the keeper to decipher. The reader of *Chinaman* is similarly placed and fascinated in following the story of cricket's finest ever but totally forgotten mystery spinner.

Romesh Gunesekera's *The Match* (2006) is the earliest of a trio of post-colonial cricket novels that, within the short space of six years at the beginning of the twenty-first century, opened up a whole new world for cricket fiction. I have left it until last because, in bringing cricket back from the post-colonial settings of *Netherland* and *Chinaman* to the metropolitan centre of the game, it suggests ways in which the world of global cricket might be brought to bear on the tradition of English cricket fiction, which has been the focus of much of this book.

First, however, a word on treating these three writers as a group. It's significant that each of them has spent the bulk of their adult life living away from their homeland. Gunesekera was born in Sri Lanka in 1954, grew up in Colombo and the Philippines and came to London in 1971 where he still lives. His years working for the British Council have involved travel to many parts of the world. Joseph O'Neill was born in Ireland a decade later, spent his early childhood in Mozambique, Turkey and Iran, and his school years in the Netherlands. He read law at Cambridge, practised as a barrister in London and later New York, where he has lived since 1998. Shehan Karunatilaka was born in Sri Lanka in 1975, spent his childhood in Colombo, had his secondary and university education in New Zealand, and has subsequently lived and worked in London, Amsterdam and Singapore

Apart from the neat symmetry of these three writers each being born a decade apart, their transient lives have exposed them to a range of different cultures, with cricket a recurring feature of their biographies. This has given each of them an outside perspective on wherever they happen to be living, a global understanding of cricket in the contemporary world and a migrant's sense of how the game can provide a way of holding on to memories of home and of coming to terms with their new life. Each of these novels also has cricket running parallel with violent political disturbance. In O'Neill's, it is 9/11, in Karunatilaka's civil war, and Gunesekera includes martial law in the Philippines, IRA activity in London and the Sri Lankan civil war in *The Match*.

Gunesekera's novel opens in Manila in 1970, seen from the point of view of teenager Sunny Fernando, whose father, Lester, a Sri Lankan journalist, has come to the Philippines, attracted by President Marcos's pledge to ensure that his country would have the freest press in Asia. Swiftly disillusioned, Lester abandons journalism while retaining some of his hopes for a region that will shake off the persisting influence of colonialism and its tainted aftermath. The prospect of cricket becoming an All-Asian game is part of this vision: 'We need it to grow in South-East Asia, the Far East. Maybe if it flourished in the Philippines, like in Australia, India, Pakistan and Ceylon, the rest of the region might take it up. Imagine Laos, Thailand, Indonesia all hitting the Brits for a six. A true game of the South'.

This gets no further than a one-day match between local ex-pats from Sri Lanka and Hong Kong, initiated by Sunny, who is obsessed with cricket. As the Sri Lankans gather for the match, insurrection is breaking out at home. The game itself is described in similar terms to those of the traditional village cricket story. A tense finish goes down to the wire, and the winning run is scored by Tina, as in *Playing Away* an updated version of the young-un, with whom Sunny is smitten. But the end of the match is also the last of cricket in the Philippines. Grenades are being let off in Manila, martial law is declared, newspapers are closed down and their editors are arrested. Within a couple of years, Sunny has left for England to study engineering.

The rest of the novel tracks Sunny's life in England from 1973 to 2002. He drops out of his engineering degree, takes a job as an accounts clerk in a department store, gets married and has a son, Mikey. His colleagues in the accounts department spend all their summer weekends 'in some green and pleasant county field', but as Sunny explains to a Philippine friend, 'It's a very exclusive game here'. Playing cricket in the home of cricket isn't easy for outsiders, as the 2023 report of the Independent Commission for Equity in Cricket (ICEC) belatedly concluded. Cricket in England and Wales, it found, 'is not a game for everyone'.

Sunny's life drifts and his interest in cricket fades. Memories of it return, however, when he visits Sri Lanka after his father's death. Hector, an old friend of his father's, takes Sunny down his garden to show him 'a big brooding tree in the corner' with a cricket ball tied to a rope still hanging from one of its branches: 'Sunny lost twenty-five years at a stroke'. As a boy he'd play here for hours on end, completely lost in a world of his own, meditatively hitting it, waiting for it to come back, hitting it again, 'Zen cricket' as he describes it. But when Hector suggests Sunny try it once more, he replies, 'Later, maybe'.

Back in London, Sunny opens a small camera shop and sets up as a family photographer. But as pics replace photos, the market for cameras falls away, and he abandons the business. His marriage goes into similar decline. Sri Lanka wins the World Cup in 1996, but Sunny is barely touched by this. It's no compensation for the carnage and terror then destroying his home country. When, half-heartedly, he tries to interest his teenage son in cricket, Mikey just shrugs: 'an MP3 player was more his thing'. The drift of the narrative anticipates aspects of *Netherland*.

Cricket, however, fills the concluding episodes of *The Match* and eases the path towards healing and reconciliation on which the novel ends. These pages centre on several matches Sunny attends in the summer of 2002. The first of these is the Lord's test in May between England and Sri Lanka. Sunny catches highlights of the first day on Channel 4 and, reminded of 'the passion of his youth', is hooked. Seeing Sri Lanka play England at Lord's is suddenly the most important thing in the world, not just for the cricket itself but because of how it might 'make his life turn the way he wanted it to, like a true spinner's ball'. He'd recently seen a flyer for a national photography competition, and the first prize of five thousand pounds would bring much-needed money to the dwindling finances of his family, restore his self-respect and revive something within him that had shrivelled.

Next morning, he sets out for Lord's with his Leica, intending to take the shot that will win him the competition. In all his years in London, he's never been to the ground. Making his way to the upper tier of the

Compton stand, he looks down at the scene, amazed at this 'green lung holding its breath every minute or so'. Gunesekera neatly captures that moment when the crowd is hushed and time, expanding slightly, holds its breath as the bowler commences their run-up. The novel's epigraph is a quotation from the French photographer Henri Cartier-Bresson – 'Shooting a picture is holding your breath' – and the prelude to the novel is titled 'Viewfinder'. Photography and cricket, shot and shot as it were, will come together in its final scenes.

But his day at Lord's is a disappointment. There are many empty seats, not many brown faces in the crowd, and the only food he can find is fish and chips, crepes or burgers – no *vadai, bola cutlis* or *lampries*. Murali is injured, and the match is heading for a tame draw. A chance meeting with Tina in the crowd is also disappointing; his early flame is no longer the person he remembered. At home that evening, watching the highlights of the day's play, Sunny realises he hasn't taken a single photo.

Nevertheless, his appetite for cricket has been whetted and reaches a climax later that summer at the Oval, at an ODI between Sri Lanka and India. The atmosphere is utterly different from the test match at Lord's. The ground is packed with South Asian supporters, and the noise is over-whelming: 'These fans had not come to watch but to participate'. An Indian cheerleader in the stand where Sunny is sitting sets up a stream of 'racy chants': anti-colonial, anti-white and anti-Pakistani. *Vadai* and pat-ties are passed along a row where a group of Sri Lankan supporters has gathered, then handed to a jovial Indian supporter who offers a crispy vegetable pakora in return. A Mexican wave starts up, 'block after block of people swaying together, leaning into the next'. Sunny joins the ripple of rising and falling bodies, caught up in the feeling they had become one. But he is still seeking his photo – 'A pure picture. The picture. Or sink'. He photographs the wave, but this isn't it.

Tendulkar unleashes a powerful drive and the ball scuds over the grass and into the midst of a flock of pigeons pecking away in the outfield. One of them is flattened. Play stops and for the first time that day the crowd is hushed. The nearest fielder picks up the bird as though it were 'the dove of peace' and carries it to the boundary. Instantly, Sunny knows this is his picture, 'a pair of clasped hands praying to a dead bird', a 'brief moment of care [...] the tender possibility of renewal'. Sri Lanka loses heavily, but Sunny leaves the ground feeling at one with the crowd and with himself. He glimpses Mikey and his girlfriend, and his sense of peace extends to include his son, for once with his father 'in the same place at the same time'. Arriving home, he finds Clara with his light metre garlanded around her neck. She'd thought he might need it and had gone to the ground to try and find him. 'I got the picture', he tells her. 'I know', she replies, 'I can see'.

One might think that cricket at this moment is bearing a weight it cannot sustain. It is not only the divisions in Sunny's life, but also those of his home country, even 'the madness infecting the rest of the world', that on this particular June afternoon seems to hold out the possibility of amity and healing. Cricket and civil war are hardly commensurate, but for Sunny the dead bird is a phoenix, 'its image rising from the strip of film and gaining a new life'. And the fact that this is probably the first treatment in fiction of an ODI, a non-traditional form of the game played in the metropolitan home of the sport between two former colonies, makes it particularly appropriate as a means of figuring oneness and transcending division.

Mike Marqusee, in an interesting review of the novel, criticised its hazy treatment of the relation between the traumas of world politics and the 'introverted consciousness' of its protagonist, focused as it is on cricket. But, like *Netherland* and *Chinaman*, the particular concern of *The Match* is with how, in the post-colonial era, cricket and its many worlds can be personally redemptive, an effective, even creative, way for the individual psyche to deal with the consequences of a displaced life. Whether or not Sunny wins the photography competition is immaterial. It's not really the prize for which Sunny is holding his breath, but a way of rescuing his life from the course it has taken. The earlier scene of the cricket ball hanging by a rope from a branch has become the hesitant prelude to his day at the Oval. Sunny's return to cricket has allowed him to find ways of rediscovering himself and reconnecting with his past.

In fact this scene did happen, except that Tendulkar's stroke was a cut, not a drive, and the bird was unharmed. And the match was indeed played in June 2002, just as Gunesekera sets it, another example of the blending of the fictive with the real, of the figurative power of cricket to offer resonance to literary fiction, and its potential for expressing concord.

Much of the interest and significance of *The Match* lies in how it brings a game that has traditionally epitomised 'Englishness' back to the old imperial centre with an entirely new cast of players. The history of those few renowned cricketers from the colonial and post-colonial world

– Ranjitsinhji, Learie Constantine, George Headley, Mansoor Ali Khan Pataudi and Imran Khan, for example – who made their mark in English cricket is well-known. But these were all famous international cricketers, most of them from elite social backgrounds, and, except for Ranjitsinhji, captains of their respective countries.

Little is known of those less celebrated cricketers from British colonies who, on either side of two world wars, made their way in the county game. As far as I can discover, there hasn't been a single history or novel devoted to the experiences of county cricketers of colour in these years. However, an article by Jo Harman in *Wisden Cricket Monthly*, 'The County Pioneers', suggests the possibilities their stories might offer. It tells of the first black West Indian to play county cricket, Charles Augustus Ollivierre, a member of the inaugural West Indian side to visit England in 1900, who remained behind after the tour and had six seasons with Derbyshire. Known as the 'Derbyshire Ranji', he played more than a hundred matches for the county while working as a clerk in a Peak District cotton mill. Harman also describes the county careers of several who followed: the Jamaican spin-bowler John Cameron, who played for Somerset in the 1930s and 1940s, for example, and another Jamaican, the all-rounder Derief Taylor, who had a long playing and coaching association with Warwickshire and also worked with the England women's team.

Immigration after the Second World War slowly increased the numbers and broadened the class background of cricketers from colonies and ex-colonies in the English county game, but there's nothing in cricket fiction and little enough in other cricket writing to show this. Lord Kitchener's famous calypso celebrating the historic victory of the touring West Indian team at Lord's in 1950 – 'Cricket, Lovely Cricket' – bore little relation to the actual experience of this new generation of immigrants in the county game. Take, for example, the unlovely incident described by Gordon Greenidge in his autobiography *The Man in the Middle* (1980). Arriving in Reading from his native island of Barbados in his early teens, Greenidge was recruited to the Hampshire ground staff in 1967. Just 17, he was soon playing for the county seconds, while also performing the standard ground staff duties of the time – cleaning dressing rooms, painting seats and helping the groundsman prepare wickets. Less standard, however, was his experience of being forcibly held while several others of the ground staff tried to smear him with whitewash. With his genitals about to be whitened, Greenidge broke free and, grabbing a spade, threatened to break it across their heads.

It's unlikely that Greenidge was the only young cricketer of colour to encounter this kind of treatment, either then or subsequently, as Azeem Rafiq's disclosures made clear and the report of the ICEC has confirmed. The story that particularly haunts me is that of Wes Stewart, a Windrush child of the 1950s, who opened the bowling for Middlesex in the late 1960s and died in 2019 after an eight-year struggle with the Home Office to avoid deportation, establish his right to British citizenship and receive the compensation to which, as one of the Windrush victims, he was entitled. Stewart's story involves an encounter with two distinct forms of hostile environment: the institutional racism of English cricket and the explicit and official racism of successive governments' immigration policies, the former taken for granted in its day, the latter an ongoing national scandal.

Stewart was born in 1945 on the northeast coast of Jamaica, famous for its Maroon communities, early nineteenth-century runaway slave settlements. At the age of 10, his family sent him to England to be raised by an older sister, a nurse. His bowling talent was spotted while playing school cricket in Tottenham, and in 1961 he joined the MCC ground staff. His duties were similar to those described by Greenidge, with one distinctive addition. Any MCC member at this time could call the Bowlers' Room for a pair of young ground staff to give them a net. Harry Latchman, the Jamaican-born leg-spinner who went on to have a successful career with Middlesex and Nottinghamshire, was a ground staff 'boy' with Stewart at this time. He described to me how tips were likely to be more generous if a member's stumps were not rearranged too often (a punitive variant of the practice we've seen in Raffles and *Pro*) but that Stewart, who loved taking wickets, would never ease off. As a result, he got less pocket money than the other bowlers. Latchman added that although neither he nor Stewart experienced the kind of treatment meted out to Greenidge, 'it was obvious that we needed to perform better than the other boys to get recognition'.

Stewart's first county season, in 1966, was highly successful: 605 overs, 164 maidens, 64 wickets at 22.42; his batting was rather less so: 17 innings, 18 runs, average 1.28. His second season also went well: 45 wickets at 23.28, the main difference from his first being that he bowled fewer overs. But things went downhill in 1968. Much of his cricket was with the Seconds, though figures of 2 for 26 off 28 overs against Yorkshire indicated that his qualities of 'straightness and length', which *Wisden* had singled out at the end of his first season, hadn't been lost. Then, at the end of the season, his contract was terminated.

His decline was startling. Another former teammate recalled that weight and fitness issues were affecting his fielding, although Stewart wouldn't have been the only opening bowler at that time to graze idly at fine leg between overs. Stewart's former wife told me that someone at the club who had been his mentor departed, leaving him without an advocate. Lonsdale Skinner, the former Surrey wicketkeeper-batter and chair of the African Caribbean Cricket Association, has identified this person as Ian Bedford, who had brought Stewart to Middlesex. Bedford, in fact, had died that year. Stewart told Skinner: 'When he died, my career died'.

There was a particular reason for Stewart's loss of form. Early in 1968, his mother in Jamaica suffered a serious stroke. The British passport Stewart had obtained as a child had by now expired, and there wasn't time to get it renewed. Instead, he was given a temporary six-week passport to visit her and reassured that if it expired while he was away, he could apply for a Jamaican passport and re-enter on that. His mother died while he was there, by which time the six-week limit had expired. However, he obtained a Jamaican passport as advised and returned to England. He hadn't been told, however, that because Jamaica had declared independence in 1962, this new passport might disqualify him from ever renewing his British one. According to Stewart's son, Wesley, his father took the death of his mother 'very hard [...] he was still crying about her ten years later'. He must have returned to London well after the 1968 season had begun, grieving for his mother and having confronted for the first time the citizenship and passport difficulties which would come to blight his final years. These factors, which must have affected Stewart's mental and physical condition, cut no ice with Middlesex when his contract was up for renewal.

Stewart continued living in north London for the next 43 years, unaware of his insecure residential status. He continued playing club cricket in north London and set up as a painter and decorator, paying his taxes and visiting Lord's whenever the West Indies were visiting. In 2011, he decided to visit Jamaica with his son to see his mother's grave and meet their remaining relatives. When he applied to the Home Office for a new passport, he was declared an illegal immigrant and, after 60 years of living in the UK assuming he was a British citizen, threatened with deportation. Thus began the nightmare of his final years.

It was only in 2018, in the wake of the Windrush scandal when a Home Office taskforce was set up to examine cases such as his, that Stewart was finally granted British citizenship. But now a further struggle with the Home Office to obtain the promised compensation, which would have paid for his obstructed visit to Jamaica, began. His British passport was finally secured early in 2019, but at the time of his sudden death 18 months later, the compensation had still not arrived. His son believes that the long years of dealing with the hostile environment administered by the Home Office had caused the stress and depression which brought about his father's death.

Stewart's is an exemplary story of the wider culture of English cricket since the Second World War, involving as it does the loss of family, place and identity that migration brought, the uncomfortable margins that the immigrant inhabited, the struggle of a talented young cricketer to sustain a career in the game and his uncertain residential status after decades of law-abiding residence and assumed citizenship in his adopted country. The significance of Stewart's story, and the ease with which a promising career disappeared, is well described by Lonsdale Skinner who in 1975 became the first black player to be capped by Surrey. When Skinner arrived in England from Guyana as a boy, 'Wes was the first black guy I saw playing cricket on the television in England [...] Three or four years later, I couldn't find him and nobody could tell me where he was. I was asking around for him for years and years'. It's not only in fiction that cricketers can entirely disappear. Stewart's story would only appear in the public domain, thanks largely to Amelia Gentleman's exposure of the Windrush scandal, five decades after his career at Middlesex had been abruptly terminated.

The narrative possibilities of stories such as Wes Stewart's or Azeem Rafiq's, and the themes they dramatize, have been neglected in fiction, as have many other significant features of the rapidly changing world of cricket. *Playing Away* was path-breaking, but the field it opened up has remained unexplored, as has the recently transformed world of women's cricket.

Children's fiction, however, sometimes goes where adult fiction is slow to venture. Moeen Ali's and Tanya Aldred's moving little story, *The Legend of Sparkhill* (2022), for example, takes some of its cues from the literary tropes and traditions this book has been exploring – there's even an idiosyncratic bowling action – while pointing in new directions. It opens with a young boy, Mo Aqeel, waking to a sunny morning with the promise of cricket in the offing, but this young-un lives in Birmingham rather than a rural village, his family is Muslim Pakistani, and his mother, after making breakfast, will be off to her job at a local retirement home. Mo's cricket team, Sparkhill, is preparing for a cup semi-final against Fenchurch, a posh team from the other side of town, the match a twenty-first-century version of the squire's team playing his estate workers. One of the stars of the Sparkhill team is Aisha, a 'wily bowler and a clever batter', but there's no changing room for her, and she has to use the girls' toilet. A close finish ends in victory for Sparkhill, after which the Fenchurch captain refuses to shake hands with Mo, telling him, 'Sparkhill stinks and most of you aren't even English'.

But the main conflict in the story concerns a clash between the additional Thursday night practice the Sparkhill coach has introduced as his team approaches the deciding cup fixtures and Mo's Arabic class, which for his parents must always come first. Tensions over availability and selection are stock-in-trade features of traditional local cricket stories, but religion versus sport is a new one. The Church of England has never stood in the way of a cricket match. The story ends on a note of resolution, as a children's story should, but rather than finding this in nostalgia for some vanishing past, it looks forward to a time when cricket will embrace diversity, perhaps even stand as a model of inclusivity in the wider national culture. Many new stories about English cricket remain to be told.

Chapter 7

ENDGAME

In a moment all was confusion. Down came a drenching rain, the cricketers dashed for cover, the lunatics began to scream, bellow and fight. One tall young man, the same B. C. Brown who had once played for Hants, pulled all his clothes off and ran about stark naked. Outside the scoring box an old man with a beard began to pray to the thunder: 'Bah! Bah! Bah!'

–Robert Graves, 'The Shout'

When an old cricketer leaves the crease
Well you never know whether he's gone
If sometimes you're catching a
Fleeting glimpse of
A twelfth man at silly mid-on.

– Roy Harper and the Grimethorpe Colliery Band

At the most general level, my aim in this book has been to trace the many different fictional scenarios into which cricket has been drawn, and to suggest how its imaginative possibilities might continue to be put to work. Paradoxically perhaps, I shall finish with the end of the world.

Robert Graves's short story, 'The Shout' (1924), is now much better known for the stylish and disturbing film version of 1978 by the Polish director Jerzy Skolimowski. Its cinematography, similar in look and feel to Robin Hardy's slightly earlier *The Wicker Man* (1973), brilliantly captures Graves's apocalyptic story of dark magic, madness and death, and makes rather more of the cricket match, set in an asylum cricket ground, that opens the story.

Two men, the anonymous frame narrator and Charles Crossley who, like the ancient mariner, will hold the other man in his narrative grip, are sitting in the score box. Crossley, described by the resident doctor as the most intelligent man in the asylum, suffers from two serious delusions: that he's killed three people in Australia, and that his soul is split into pieces. As the cricket gets underway, the frame narrator keeps the score while Crossley tells his story, a story that he says is true, that he's told many times before but always in a new way. It's the variation that keeps it true, he explains; otherwise, it would drag and become false.

The heart, or better perhaps the soul, of Crossley's story is his magic shout learnt from 'the chief devil of the Northern Territory'. It has two degrees: the first which terrifies and the second which kills. It has taken him 18 years to perfect, and he's used it no more than five times, whether of the first or second kind we're not told. Crossley has been staying at the nearby home of a couple, Richard and Rachel, upon whom he's quietly forced himself. His shout, he's explained to Richard, is one of pure evil, pure terror: 'There is no fixed place for it on the scale. It may take any note.' He takes Richard deep into the neighbouring sand hills to demonstrate.

Richard, thoroughly scared, waits at shouting distance from Crossley and blocks his ears. Crossley leans oddly forward, chin thrust out, teeth bared:

> His face […] usually soft and changing, uncertain as a cloud, now hardened to a rough stone mask, dead white at first, and then flushing outwards from the cheek bones red and redder, and at last as black, as if he were about to choke. His mouth then slowly opened to the full, and Richard fell on his face, his hands to his ears, in a faint.

It's here that the story most needs the film. Alan Bates's grimace and roar are unearthly beyond description.

Although in the course of his narrative Crossley occasionally comes out of the main story and back to the score box, the cricket is not seen again until the end. The film, however, cuts back to the cricket several times. Crossley's shout is echoed by one of the inmates appealing for an lbw with a roar as blood-curdling and prolonged as Stuart Broad's in full voice. His response to the appeal being turned down might also suggest Broad. He stares furiously at the umpire, a nurse from the asylum, and begins to chant 'Out! Out! Out!', a cry then taken up by all the fielders.

The motif of the shout which echoes through Skolimowski's film is amplified by a reproduction of Francis Bacon's 1949 painting of a screaming pope, 'Head vi', on the wall of Richard's sound studio (he's a composer experimenting with natural sounds). Bacon's painting, in its turn, was inspired by the image of the screaming nurse in Eisenstein's famous 1925 film *Battleship Potemkin*. And just one year before this, Graves's strange and wonderful story. What a distinguished line of influence leading to Stuart Broad.

The story and the film end in mayhem like no other in cricket fiction. A violent electrical storm breaks, and as the visiting cricketers dash for cover, the patients take over the asylum. They scream, bellow and fight, one of them pulls off his clothes and runs about brandishing a stump in each hand. The thunder intensifies. The doctor breaks into the score box and orders Crossley back to the dormitory. He refuses, they struggle and Crossley threatens to shout the asylum down. They're both struck dead by lightning. The film, though not Graves's story, ends with Crossley and a number of dead cricketers laid out on tables in the asylum dining room like so many David Warners. Both story and film, however, show cricket at the end-times. The asylum is the antithesis of the placid village green, and the film concludes with a morgue-like tableau of rows of dead cricketers.

R. C. Sherriff's novel *The Hopkins Manuscript* (1939), although very different in mode, extrapolates this picture onto a world scale. Sherriff is best-known for his First World War play *Journey's End* (1928), a work that prompted a flood of writing about the war a decade on, as if memories of the trenches had hitherto been repressed. He also wrote screenplays for films such as *The Invisible Man, Goodbye Mr Chips* and *The Dam Busters*.

The Hopkins Manuscript is set in the small Hampshire village of Beadle as it prepares for the end. The moon has veered off course and will collide with Earth on 3 May 1946. The story is told by a retired school teacher who has survived the cataclysm, written an account of the disaster, sealed it in a thermos flask and hidden it among the ruins of London. One thousand years later, it has been discovered by archaeologists from the Royal Society of Abyssinia. The moon had crashed into the Atlantic, destroying Western civilisation though not the colonised world. The archaeologists describe Edwin Hopkins's manuscript as 'a thin lonely cry of anguish from the gathering darkness of dying England'. The only other remains they have found is a 'Keep off the Grass' sign which has been deciphered and lodged in the Royal Collection in Addis Ababa. Sherriff has his fun, but the novel is deadly serious, recalling H. G. Wells' *In the Days of the Comet* (1906) in which the world also watches and waits for the arrival of a cosmic visitor portending the end of the world.

Hopkins, Sherriff's narrator, is a stuffy, touchy, pedantic middle-aged man whose life before the imminent threat from the moon has been devoted to his prize-winning poultry. Pondering how he should fill the seven months before the cataclysm, he decides to read all 30 volumes of the collected works of Sir Walter Scott. There's gentle comedy here, a narrator reminiscent of Mr Pooter in George and Weedon Grossmith's comic novel *The Diary of a Nobody* (1892), but one whose laborious eye for detail and fussy interaction with the world of his village captures the social psychology of a small community facing destruction.

Beadle must keep itself occupied as it waits for the moon. The main diversion as the moon comes closer and grows larger is the construction of an underground shelter where the villagers will retreat on 3 May. Hopkins, rather to his own surprise, enthusiastically joins in this project. But the shelter is finished several days before the critical date and so, to fill the little time that's left and divert the villagers, a moonlight cricket match between the married and single men of Beadle is organised for 1 May, to begin at 9 p.m. with stumps to be drawn at midnight. A marquee is erected, the canvas sight-screens are put up, the players assemble and the village turns out to watch.

Hopkins dislikes cricket and has never before bothered to attend village matches, but this match is like no other, 'a farewell ceremony to the game that had graced the meadows and greens of England for so many years'. As the cricket begins, the moon,

> hung like a great amber, pock-marked lamp above a billiard table, so vast and enveloping that the little white-clad cricketers moved without shadows to their appointed places on the field.

For a while, 'the ghastly menace of that calm night' is forgotten 'as the magic of the game' absorbs the crowd. The squire watches proudly as his young nephew, Robin, walks to the wicket 'in immaculate white flannels [...] wearing the striped cap of his House Eleven [...] as any boy might walk to open the batting for his school at Lord's'.

But as the moon's 'dazzling splendour' wanes to a reddish glow and then a dusty brown, a thunderstorm breaks over the ground. Cricket caps are whisked off into the sky, and the marquee is swept away. The storm passes as quickly as it came, but the light is now almost completely extinguished. It is the time of the endgame. The players pack up their gear and make their way to the shelter or their homes to wait. The squire departs with his nephew, Robin's leather-handled cricket bag carried between them.

There are new dark sides for cricket fiction to explore. The coming world of cricket anticipated in *Slow Turn* and *Netherland* is refashioning the English game to make it scarcely recognisable as the one discussed in the earlier chapters of this book. The global spread of major league cricket franchises and the outsourcing of the English Hundred franchises to private equity investors such as a Silicon Valley consortium including the chief executives of Microsoft and Google, and to Indian Premier League owners, are transforming English cricket utterly. Professional cricketers, as the cricket journalist Ali Martin has suggested, are becoming more like tennis or golf pros with their own managers, coaches and support staff, citizens of the cricket world, of everywhere and nowhere, every game an away game. Will the Ashes, he wonders, become a standalone event like the Ryder Cup? The forces driving all this seem irresistible and not wholly deplorable. Who can disagree with Dave Stott's description of county cricket? But the consequences for cherished aspects of English cricket will spell the end-of-days for many of the features that have long defined it.

Unequivocally worse than this, sports capitalism is hastening a different kind of endgame. As the world floods and burns, cricket's contribution to the relentless process of climate crisis – the air miles, the sponsorship of fossil fuel companies, the energy consumption and carbon emissions of the global game – will remorselessly contribute to the destruction of our planet. It has been a long time now since a cricket ground was, as described in *Alibi Innings*, 'a charmed space, an isolated piece of England with the vast, loud, dangerous world outside shut off for an hour or two'.

Cricket has always been one of the few sports where results are frequently determined by weather, but global heating, with its whiplash between extreme wet and extreme dry conditions, has made it the most vulnerable of all major pitch sports. Repeated flooding is forcing grounds to be abandoned. Players are sometimes collapsing at the wicket because of extreme temperatures. Heat, as well as rain, will become a reason for abandoning play. The drop-in pitches and practice strips used at the T20 World Cup in 2024, intended to ensure wickets with pace and consistent bounce and sown with grass suited to hotter climates, were transported 14,000 miles by shipping container from Adelaide to Florida and New York. And still the bounce was uneven.

Severe storms that killed over twenty people and destroyed parts of the Grand Prairie ground in Texas, where the official warm-up game of the tournament was to take place, forced it to be cancelled. Consequently, the opening match of the tournament at the same ground a week later – between the United States and Canada, a 'replay' of the first-ever international match in 1844 – had to be powered by temporary generators. The short- and long-term costs of the showpiece match of the tournament between India and Pakistan in New York (Chuck's vision made real) were neatly summed up by the *Guardian* journalist Andy Bull: five years of planning, six months of construction work, a security operation involving the police forces of three countries and the FBI, police snipers, roadblocks, helicopters, a 50-person video surveillance team and the closure of 1,000 acres of public park.

The money flooding into English cricket from investments such as those outlined above has been described by the chief executive of the English and Wales Cricket Board as recapitalising the county game and sustaining it for the next 20 to 25 years. Capitalisation alone will not sustain cricket and could well contribute to its demise. Cricket, as Ned Vessey has tersely described it, is 'nine wickets down'. Perhaps the latest and bleakest of all cricket stories will be the game's tragic and contradictory endeavour to expand and survive.

BIBLIOGRAPHY

Ali, Moen & Aldred, Tanya, *The Legend of Sparkhill* (London: Fairfield Books, 2022)

Barrie, J.M., *The Greenwood Hat* (London: Peter Davies Ltd., 1937)

Bateman, Anthony, *Cricket, Literature and Culture: Symbolising the Nation, Destabilising Empire* (London: Routledge, 2016)

Bateman, Anthony & Hill, Jeffrey, eds., *The Cambridge Companion to Cricket* (Cambridge: Cambridge University Press, 2011)

Benson, E.F., *David Blaize* (London: The Hogarth Press, 1989)

Blake, Nicholas, *A Question of Proof* (London: Vintage Books, 2021)

Bright-Holmes, John, ed., *Lords & Commons: Cricket in Novels and Stories* (London: Andre Deutsch, 1988)

Brearley, Mike, *Turning Over the Pebbles*: *A Life in Cricket and in the Mind* (London: Constable, 2023)

Bull, Andy, 'Pakistan Stumble in Tight Chase Amid Merry Chaos of Showpiece', *Guardian,* 10 June 2024

Buruma, Ian, *Playing the Game* (London: Jonathan Cape, 1991)

Carr, J.L., *A Season in Sinji* (Bury St. Edmunds: The Quince Tree Press, 2003)

Chan, Wilfrid, 'Power Play: New York Cricketers and ICC Face Off Over World Cup Plan', *The Guardian*, 2 September 2023

Davie, Michael & Davie, Simon, eds., *The Faber Book of Cricket* (London: Faber & Faber, 1987)

De Selincourt, Hugh, *The Cricket Match* (Oxford: Oxford University Press, 1987)

Dexter, Ted & Makins, Clifford, *Testkill* (Harmondworth: Penguin Books, 1976)

Dickens, Charles, *The Pickwick Papers* (London: Oxford University Press, 1964)

Doyle, Arthur Conan, *The Story of Spedegue's Dropper and other Cricketing Miscellanea* (Tunbridge Wells: Solis Press, 2016)

Edmond, Rod, 'Joseph Wells – A Victorian Round-Arm', *The Nightwatchman* 22, Summer 2018

Edmond, Rod, '"An Unmade Bed of a Man": Simon Raven and Cricket', *The Nightwatchman* 25, Spring 2019

Edmond, Rod, 'The Rise and Fall of the Village Cricket Story', *The Nightwatchman* 37, Spring 2022

Forster, E.M, *Maurice* (London: Penguin Books, 2005)

Frith, David, *Silence of the Heart: Cricket Suicides* (Edinburgh & London: Mainstream Publishing, 2001)

Gentleman, Amelia, *The Windrush Betrayal: Exposing the Hostile Environment* (London: Guardian Faber, 2020)

Graves, Robert, *The Shout and Other Stories* (Harmondswoth: Penguin Books, 1964)

Green, Benny, *P.G. Wodehouse: A Literary Biography* (London: Michael Joseph, 1981)

Gunesekera, Romesh, *The Match* (London: Bloomsbury, 2006)

Hamilton, Bruce, *Pro: An English Tragedy* (London: The Cresset Press, 1946)

Harman, Jo, 'The County Pioneers', *Wisden Cricket Monthly* 41, March 2021

Harman, Jo, 'Greener Futures Series', *Wisden Cricket Monthly* 79, 2024 & ff.

Hartley, L.P., *The Go-Between* (London: Penguin Modern Classics, 2020)

Hay, Ian, *Pip: A Romance of Youth* (London: William Blackwood, 1907)

Hornung, E.W., *Raffles: The Amateur Cracksman* (London: Penguin Books, 2003)

Hornung, E.W., *Raffles: Further Adventures of the Amateur Cracksman* (Ashed Phoenix Library, 2018)

Hughes, Thomas, *Tom Brown's Schooldays* (Oxford: World's Classics, 2008)

James, C.L.R., *Beyond A Boundary* (London: Hutchinson, 1969)

Joyce, James, *A Portrait of the Artist as a Young Man* (London: Jonathan Cape, 1941)

Joyce, James, *Ulysses* (London: Penguin Books, 1992)

Joyce, James, *Finnegans Wake* (New York: The Viking Press, 1973)

Karunatilaka, Shehan, *Chinaman: The Legend of Pradeep Mathew* (London: Vintage Books, 2012)

Macdonell, A.G., *England, Their England* (Fonthill Media, 2012)

Martin, Ali, 'Test Cricket's Future is Complex', *Observer*, 26 May 2024

Marqusee, Mike, *Slow Turn* (London: Michael Joseph, 1988)

Marqusee, Mike, *Anyone But England* (London: Aurum Press, 1994)

Marqusee, Mike, *War Minus the Shooting* (London: Mandarin, 1996)

Marqusee, Mike, Review of Romesh Gunesekera, *The Match*, *Guardian Review*, 11 March, 2006

Masterman, J.C., *Fate Cannot Harm Me* (London: Victor Gollancz, 1931)

Midwinter, Eric, *Quill on Willow: Cricket in Literature* (Chichester: Aeneas Press, 2001)

Mitchell, Alan W., *Cricket Companions: The Story of the 1949 New Zealand Tour* (London: Werner Laurie, 1950)

Mitford, Mary Russell, 'A Country Cricket Match', *Lady's Magazine*, July 1823

Nandy, Ashis, *The Tao of Cricket* (Harmondsworth: Penguin Books, 1989)

Nicholson. Rafaelle, *Ladies and Lords: A History of Women's Cricket in Britain* (London: Peter Lang, 2019)

O'Neill, Joseph, *Netherland* (London: Fourth Estate, 2009)

Parker, John, *The Village Cricket Match* (Harmondsworth: Penguin Books, 1987)

Phillips, Caryl, *Playing Away* (London: Faber & Faber, 1987)

Quinn, Anthony, *Half of the Human Race* (London: Vintage Books, 2012)

Radford, E. & M.A., *Murder Isn't Cricket* (London: Dean Street Press, 2019)

Raven, Simon, *Fielding Gray* (London: Vintage Books, 2012)

Raven, Simon, *Shadows on the Grass* (Cornwall: House of Stratus, 2001)

Raymond, Ernest, *Tell England: A Study in a Generation* (reprinted in Great Britain by Amazon, nd.)

Richards, Dylan, 'Woolf at the Wicket', *The Nightwatchman* 44, Winter 2003

Rogers, Byron, *The Last Englishman: The Life of J.L. Carr* (London: Aurum Press, 2003)

Sassoon, Siegfried, *Memoirs of a Fox-Hunting Man* (London: Faber & Faber, 1975)

Sayers, Dorothy L., *Murder Must Advertise* (London: Hodder, 2016)

Sherriff, R.C., *The Hopkins Manuscript* (London: Victor Gollancz,1939)

Spain, Nancy, *Death Before Wicket* (London: Hutchinson, 1946)

Spain, Nancy, *Why I'm Not a Millionaire: An Autobiography* (London: Hutchinson, 1956)

Stevenson, R.L., *The Strange Case of Dr Jekyll and Mr Hyde* (London: Penguin Books, 1979)

Swanton, E.W., ed., *Best Cricket Stories* (London: The Sportsmans Book Club, 1963)

Telfer, Kevin, *Peter Pan's First XI: The Extraordinary Story of J.M. Barrie's Cricket Team* (London: Sceptre, 2010)

Timms, Aaron, 'Can cricket crack America? New T20 League Aims to Take US by Storm', *The Guardian*, 12 July 2023

Vachell, H.A., *The Hill* (Los Angeles: Viewforth Press, 2011)

Vessey, Ned, 'A Green Game', *The Nightwatchman* 42, Summer 2023

Waugh, Alec, *The Loom of Youth* (London: Methuen, 1984)

Wells, H.G., 'The Veteran Cricketer', in *Certain Personal Matters* (Forgotten Books, 2016)

Wells, H.G., *Experiment in Autobiography* (London: Victor Gollancz, 1934)

Willans, Geoffrey & Searle, Ronald, *Molesworth: How to be Topp* (London: Penguin Books, 1999)

Williams, Jack, *Cricket and England*: *A Cultural and Social History of the Inter-War Years* (London: Frank Cass, 2003)

Wodehouse, P.G., *Wodehouse at the Wicket*, ed. Murray Hedgcock (London: Arrow Books, 2011)

Wodehouse, P.G., *Mike and Psmith* (Aeterna, nd.)

Woodcock, David, The Story of Cricket in 50 Books series, *Wisden Cricket Monthly* 74, 2024 & ff

Woolf, Virginia, *Mrs Dalloway* (London: Penguin Books, 1992)

Worsley, T.C., *Flannelled Fool* (London: The Hogarth Press, 1985)

Worsley-Gough, Barbara, *Alibi Innings* (Harmondsworth: Penguin Books, 1958)

ACKNOWLEDGEMENTS

My thanks to the editors of *The Nightwatchman* for permission to include material from several essays of mine they have published – on the village cricket story, Joseph Wells and Simon Raven. See the bibliography for full details.

Thanks also to the team at Anthem Press.

Warm and particular thanks to those who have, through conversation, advice and friendship, helped in the making of this book: Steve Bates, David Ellis, David Flusfeder, Abdulrazak Gurnah, Jon Hotten, Lyn Innes, David Kynaston, Ian Marshall, Jan Montefiore, Gill Perry, Matt Thacker, Scarlett Thomas, Michael Turnbull, Phil Walker, Dennis Walder. Each of you, in various ways, exemplifies the truth of C. L. R. James's wise remark: 'What do they know of cricket who only cricket know.'

And most broadly, but still pertinently, my thanks to all the various cricket teams – too many to name or even remember – I have played with, from Forest Lake Primary School 1952 to Walmer Cricket Club 2024.

INDEX

www.ingramcontent.com/pod-product-compliance
Ingram Content Group UK Ltd.
Pitfield, Milton Keynes, MK11 3LW, UK
UKHW041858031125
464644UK00003B/14